DIRTY LITTLE PSYCHO

SINNERS WELCOME

SAMANTHA BARRETT

DEDICATION

*I know you've read the first three books and the fact
you picked this one up means...
You are going to be joining me in hell.
Don't worry, babes, at least we'll get fucked by the
devil and have our asses spanked daily.*

P.S...

*Stop wasting God's time and having him listen to
your prayers when you know you will sin again.*

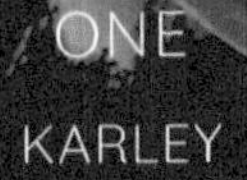

ONE

KARLEY

"I am going to ruin all of your fucking lives!" I scream as they slam the door closed. I rush forward and beat my fists against it. "Motherfuckers!"

"It's soundproof." I whirl around in fright, I had no idea anyone else was in here. The sight of him sitting there on the edge of the bed, with his arms casually resting on the tops of his thighs, has me tensing from surprise. I snort at the sight of him wearing the same blue scrubs as me, standard uniform around here I guess. His brown eyes drink in the sight of me. When he pushes to his feet, my eyes snap wide at the sheer size of him. He's at least two feet taller than me, tattoos covering his forearms. I can just make out the skulls before my attention is darted back to his face.

I press my back flat against the door and scowl at the fucker. "Stay the hell where you are!" I warn. He ignores me and eliminates the space between us, my breath hitching when he places his hands on either side of my head and cages me in. He tips his head down and his black hair flops onto his forehead, the strange urge to brush the strands back comes over me but I force my hands to remain at my sides.

"You're in my world now. Best to remember that when you start running that pretty little mouth of yours."

I swallow audibly and keep my terror from splaying on my face and I meet his dark stare with one of my own. "Boy, please, the shadows are my friends and I plan to cause as much mayhem as I can while I'm here."

His eyes take on a calculating edge. "Why are you in the men's wing? You shouldn't be in here with me. Get out," he snarls, then pushes back and darts across the room and huddles in the corner. I stare at him in stupor.

"Do you really think I would still be standing here if there was a fucking way out?" I snap.

"If you don't get the fuck out of here in the next three minutes, you'll become my new toy."

Against my will I shiver at the innuendo.

Fucking one of the inmates would be a surefire way to piss the old bastard off and send his ass to an early grave. His eyes narrow to slits when I smile seductively and I reach up to twirl my black hair around my finger.

"I mean..." I let my sentence trail off. His growl should have me dropping to my knees and begging to get the hell out of here, but instead all I feel is the need to push him. Shit, maybe there is something wrong with me after all. I've been in here two minutes, have no idea what the hell this guy's name is and yet I'm ready to let him fuck me, just so I can send the old man over the edge. I drop my arms back to my sides and huff out an annoyed breath. "I don't see another way out, can you just... not break me?"

His eyes narrow and his nostrils flare as he presses back against the concrete wall, almost like he is fighting against himself to remain where he is and not come at me. For the first time since I was dragged out of my room and brought here against my will, I feel a sliver of fear and I despise that feeling. Unknowingly I take a tentative step backward and raise my hands as if surrendering.

"You have forty-five minutes before the doors open, when that happens, don't run. Back out of the room slowly and then get as far away from this room as you can."

I bite back my snort. "You make it sound like you're some kind of predator," I say, trying to lighten the tension in this cell. When his eyes darken and his upper lip pulls back in a snarl, I swallow loudly.

"I'm the worst kind of predator and you would be wise to remember that. Follow my instructions and you just might make it out of here tonight *intact*." I clamp my mouth closed and slowly back away until I'm in the opposite corner, heeding his warning and never turning my back. I press against the concrete wall and glide down until I'm sitting on the cold floor. He mimics my move and eyes me with such scrutiny I have to fight not to fidget.

I mull over his words and then hyperfocus on one part. "What did you mean *the doors will open?*" I ask.

A cruel smirk graces his handsome face. "Slade Le Roux isn't just an asylum for the unhinged and mentally disturbed, it is a place where people with the darkest kind of desires are sent to be cleansed. The chaplain thought he could cure us all of our ungodly ways, but that fucker has been corrupted and is now one of us."

Fear grips me in its clutches. "What happens

when the door opens?" The slight tremble in my voice pisses me off but I would be lying if I said I wasn't fearful of his answer. He steps forward toward the metal cot, with a mattress that looks thinner than a bed sheet, and pushes the single threadbare blanket to the side and lifts a mask. My brows leap to my hairline at the sight of the bright red mask, thick black lines reaching from the top to the bottom of the eye parts, but it's the devil horns atop it that have my breaths coming in fast pants. The mask is old and the paint looks like it is peeling, which just adds to the ominous appearance of it all.

His gaze slowly lifts to mine and the excited look in those brown eyes sets my blood pressure rising. "We hunt." I suck a sharp inhale at his declaration, something tells me he isn't talking about hunting wild game.

I shake my head, trying to deny his claim. I'm a ballsy bitch and will hold my own against any fucker, but something about this place and the danger that clings to my new cellmate has put me on edge. I'm at a disadvantage here and I hate it. I retie my shoelaces and make sure they are done up tight, then gather my black hair and secure it in a ponytail. I have no idea what awaits me when that damn door opens but I won't be caught off guard.

I draw my knees up and rest my arms over the top of them as I stare at the sexy, unhinged bastard across from me.

"Any pointers on where I should hide until they lock the doors again?"

"The doors remain open until sunrise. Nowhere is off limits. The entire facility is fenced and we have free reign until daylight. Run, don't stop."

I snort. "That's real fucking helpful," I bite out.

"When the devils come for the prey there is no escape. The torture they inflict is depraved and sinister. No amount of prayers to your make-believe God will make them stop." His words send a shiver down my spine.

Time seems to tick by faster than I had hoped. When he starts pulling his mask on, I push to my feet and keep my back against the wall as I edge toward the door, waiting for the moment the lock disengages and I can escape this madness and find a way out of this fucking hellhole. I close my eyes and try to calm my nerves by giving myself a mental pep talk. When I finally open them again, a scream lodges in my throat as he's standing directly in front of me with that mask on. His eyes look almost black but there is no mistaking the desire swirling in their depths as he gazes down at me.

When he reaches out and grips my ponytail, tugging on it, a whimper escapes me. "I'm going to enjoy breaking you, beauty." His words are quietly spoken but delivered with the force of a punch to the gut.

I knew my dad was a crazy bastard, but I never thought he would stick me in another one of these places. Now I'm going to have to run for my life before the devils catch me.

TWO

CARTER

"Forgiveness will never be granted but it won't stop me from asking you for it each night. I may not be deserving of it but I want it nonetheless." I may have turned my back on my faith and allowed this place to sink its dark claws into me, but that doesn't mean I want to burn for eternity in the afterlife. I long for the depravity this place offers. The moment I stepped foot on these tainted grounds, I knew my faith would be shaken.

When I peer down at my watch and see it's 11:58 p.m. I smile. Pushing to my feet, I cross the damp concrete cell and retrieve my mask from the edge of the bed. It's a pure matte black devil's mask but unlike the ones you see in stores my horns curve outward and stretch upward. There may be three of us and we all wear the masks, but you will never know which one is which as we love to switch shit up. I slip my mask on just as the buzzer sounds, signaling the opening of the doors.

I pull the door open, ready to step out, but jerk backward when a blur of black hair sprints past me like her ass is on fire. I step out of the cell and stare after her until I feel a presence at my side. I turn to see Draven standing there.

"I found us a new toy to play with." The dark excitement in his tone has me grinning behind my mask.

"We hunting?" I ask with an edge to my voice.

"Fuck yeah, let's get Vaughn." I nod and follow after him. All the other patients dart out of our way when they see us coming. We are the lords of this palace and these fuckers know it. A few of them have tried to take the power from us but they learned quickly that we aren't the ones to fuck with. We have no qualms about breaking them or making their deaths look like a suicide. In here, we make the rules.

Don't harm the staff.
Return to your cells by sunrise
No rape.
All participants must be willing.
Break the rules and we'll break your face.

When we reach where Vaughn usually stands, he's not there. I look to Draven. "Bet you she ran past, triggered his hunter instinct and he followed her."

I nod, knowing he's probably right. Vaughn loves hunting his prey and stalking it until he drives them out of their mind with fear before he finally strikes.

"Outside." Draven nods and follows after me. We're an unlikely trio given all of our pasts. The only one who is *meant* to be in here, I use that term *meant* loosely because I don't think there is anything fucking wrong with him, Draven. He's been stuck in here for the better part of four years and this place has done nothing to quell his urges, if anything it has only enhanced them.

Vaughn is just as fucked up as I am.

There is no other way to explain it. The difference between me and Vaughn compared to Draven is the fact we were employed by Slade Le Roux once. Well, Vaughn technically still is.

The moment we exit the back of the building, we spot Vaughn standing there in the middle of the washed-out basketball court, the concrete cracked, the hoops on both ends rusted and broken. Why they have a court here is a fucking joke, considering they don't even have any balls for the inmates to play with. At the sound of our approach, he turns to face us, his purple devil mask shimmering under the moonlight. Unlike both mine and Draven's, Vaughn's has cracks through the whole thing, his horns snapped in half, which only adds to the dark allure of his mask.

We come to stand by his side. "You found Draven's new toy?" I ask.

The fucker chuckles and nods, then points across the yard toward the boundary fence. We follow his direction and join him in laughter when we see Draven's new toy stomping in frustration. "How did you find her?" Vaughn asks him.

"She was put in my cell." Both Vaughn and I snap our heads toward him. No one is permitted into Draven's cell. Being put into his cell is a death sentence for your ass or in her case, her pussy. This is an all-male facility. Having a female in here is going to stir some fucking shit up.

"You didn't tell her the fence was electric, did you?" I press.

The sinister fucker just laughs. "Where the fuck would the fun be in that?" he answers. Vaughn and I just shake our heads. If this girl thought she was being put into a cell with a gentleman, then she is sorely mistaken. The only kind thing about Draven is that he'll offer to use lube before he slams his monster cock in your ass.

"Motherfucker!" she screams when she is zapped by the fence again. She flings her hands around, trying to ward off the pain. She still hasn't noticed our presence.

"Split up?" I ask.

"Take her to the basement and let's have some fun," Vaughn adds.

"I want to test her limits," Draven adds.

"Draven, you can't break her, you know the rules," I warn.

He growls. "She'll be begging for my cock, I guarantee that."

"We'll see," Vaughn says, beginning to dart away. I go in the opposite direction, leaving Draven to take the front on approach. The fucker will act salty but we all know Draven will love the shocked expression when she sees him. I spot Vaughn as he slips behind a tree and uses it for cover while I stay plastered against the side of the building, in the shadows, waiting for Draven to make his move. We've done this move plenty of times when other inmates decided to try and push our rules.

Excitement is coursing through me like a wave, it's been a long time since we have had fun. Most of our nights are spent patrolling the inmates and keeping order. On some nights, when a fight breaks out, we get to release our demons and those nights... fuck, those nights are the nights I crave. The blood-lust, the haze of euphoric bliss that overtakes each of us as we dole out the punishment is perfection, but it's what comes after that, *that* tips us right over the fucking edge.

Covered in the blood of our victims, we fuck each other like savages. It's rough, dirty, wrong and oh so fucking filthy, but goddamnit, we fucking crave the high. The three of us may fuck and share a bond built from need but we love fucking harder than most. These two are my brothers. We may not be committed in a relationship but make no fucking mistake, we are committed to each other and will remain that way until the end of fucking time.

This new toy Draven has found will hold our focus for a night or two, like all the others, before we get bored and go back to tormenting each other's cocks.

"Oh, my little beauty is a bit of psycho, isn't she?" At the sound of Draven's voice she tenses, then slowly turns to face him. He looks like an unhinged fucker standing there in his black clothing and mask, the moon as the only lighting out here. It casts an eerie glow over him, making him appear like the devil him-fucking-self.

If only she knew there are two more sinners lurking in the shadows, waiting to release our demons on her.

THREE

KARLEY

My breath hitches at the sight of him. He told me to run the moment the door opened and I did. I high-tailed it the fuck out of there and shoved every cunt out of my way that tried to stop me. I thought going out the back I would be able to scale the fence and escape this shithole, then make it back home to stab my father in the fucking eye for daring to put me in this place!

What I didn't fucking bank on was the fence being electric!

The first zap sent me sailing backward and I landed on my ass. I thought being prepared for the zap the second time would help me brace for it, but turns out being electrocuted twice in a short span of time hurts more!

I dart my gaze around, trying to spot another way out, but it's too fucking dark out to see anything clearly. When he begins stalking toward me, I start to panic, my mind screaming at me to run but my body is begging for me to stay. If the pulse between my legs is anything to go by, then my slutty little clitty is begging for some action from the psycho.

"You run, we chase," he warns.

A frown pulls at my brows. "*We?*" I breathe out.

I may not be able to see his face but I can hear the smile in his voice when he speaks. "Yeah little psycho, *we.*"

He's mere feet away from me and I need to make a choice. I ignore my body's reaction to the fear—I'm a freak, I get off on being terrified. I dart to the side and head toward the trees. I have no idea how deep I can go before I undoubtedly hit another fence, but I'm not going to stand and let him get his hands on me. I make it past the first tree only to slam into something. I cry out and fall to my ass. I reach up and rub my nose, angry I didn't see the second tree. I try to push to my feet but I'm shoved down.

I snap my head upward, my jaw slackening at the sight of another masked freak standing in front of me. Something about this masked fucker has fear rearing inside me. I scoot backward along the ground, only to be stopped when my back hits something else. I tilt my head back and lock eyes with the crazy fucker from before.

"You said to run!" I snap at him.

The bastard shrugs his shoulders. "I never said you would get away." That's all he says before he reaches down, grips my ponytail, using it to haul me to my feet. I cry out in pain, but he ignores me as he drags me back toward the building. I swing my arms out and try to fight but his grip on my hair makes it impossible for me to escape. I hear the other bastard trailing behind us and my fear begins to grow to new heights. I loathe the fact that my pussy is pounding to the beat of its own damn drum right now.

I feel strands of my hair ripping out but my cries and pleas are falling on deaf ears. The guy behind us darts in front and pulls the door to the building open. When he tries to drag me through, I grip the sides of the doorframe, trying to fight against him even when he tugs on my ponytail. When I feel the one behind me flush against my back, I stop fighting and the other one stops pulling on my hair.

I shiver when I feel the plastic of his mask press against the side of my face. "I can't wait to fuck the devil into you." His words have a gasp falling from my lips. The other guy uses my moment of distraction to his advantage and tugs me forward. I stumble after him, trying my hardest not to lag behind and risk him tearing more of my hair out.

I'm a fucking fool for thinking he would let me go. I thought his warning back in the cell gave me hope that I might actually escape this place, but those hopes went up in flames the moment I realized the fence was electric.

I follow him down some stairs and pray I don't fall, the lighting is pathetic to say the least. Once we reach the bottom he releases me. I flick my hair back and whirl around to try and find an escape, but freeze on the spot when I realize where the fuck they have brought me. I feel one of them press against my back, this time I shiver for a different reason—fear.

"Don't worry, little psycho, I'm not planning on locking you in one of those." His words do nothing to quell the anxiety rising inside me as I stand here and stare at the mortuary chambers. There are three metal tables that are vacant, thank God for small fucking mercies. This place looks like something from a horror movie, and my stomach rolls.

They're going to kill me.

My father sent me here to teach me a lesson. I

wonder if he knew that this place would be the death of me?

"Why are you doing this?" I whisper, fear lacing each of my words, and I can't find it within myself to care. I'm terrified and disgusted with myself that I will die while my panties are soaked.

"Because I want to see inside you." I whimper at his words. "I want to see your terror. I want to know what breaks you."

I peer over my shoulder at him, his brown eyes are focused on me with an intensity I can't explain. "Why?" I breathe out. Tears prick the backs of my eyes, but I refuse to give these bastards the satisfaction of seeing any more of my tears.

It isn't him that answers, it's the guy who I slammed into who does. "Haven't you ever had dark desires that you hid from the world for fear you would be judged?" I swallow audibly and shake my head.

"Liar." I whirl around and jerk back into the guy behind me as I stare at another masked freak in front of me.

There are three of them!

My heart rate spikes as the one behind me wraps his arms around my waist, anchoring me to him. My vocal cords fail me when the newcomer stalks toward us. I should scream, fight or try to flee, but I do none of that. What's the point? I've already been warned that I'm on my own until sunrise, I doubt I'll survive that fucking long if these three have anything to do with it. When I feel the heat of his body pressed against my front I close my eyes and wait.

His fingers grip my chin and force my head up. "Open your eyes, beauty." Like a moth to a fucking flame I obey the new guy. His blue eyes stand out like a bright light against his matte black mask with large horns. "Death is a mercy we are not granted for many years. Yours will not be from our hands unless you break the rules."

My brows slam together in confusion. "You're not going to kill me?"

He shakes his head. "Unless you break our rules," he answers.

"What rules?"

"Don't harm the staff. Return to your cell by sunrise. No rape. All participants must be willing. Break the rules and we'll break your face," the three of them all say in unison. I mull over their words and when they sink in my eyes widen.

"No rape?"

The one I slammed into moves until he is standing behind the one in front of me, drawing my sole focus to him. "We'll never take what isn't freely given."

Curse my fucking pussy, the dirty bitch begins to throb again at the thought of giving these three my body willingly. What would they do? Would they bring me pleasure like I have never known before?

FOUR

DRAVEN

She's acting scared.

I can feel her resistance slowly easing, knowing that we will never take what she isn't willing to give. She melts against me without knowing it. I feel a shiver roll down her spine at Vaughn's words. She gets off on this shit as much as we do. The morgue in this place hasn't been used in years, she doesn't need to know that though.

"Tonight, we're going to test your limits. Your mouth may say *no* but your body will be the one to speak the truth," Carter says.

"Your body speaks to us, not your mouth. Break that rule and we'll be forced to gag you," I add. She sucks in a sharp inhale and surprises the fuck out of me by nodding. It's been years since I've been able to taste or even touch a pussy. The thought of being able to slide my tongue through her folds and taste her arousal has my cock growing rock hard. The second she feels it she gasps and tries to pull free of my hold, but I refuse to allow her to move.

"Let the games begin," Vaughn says as he stalks toward the metal slab in the middle. Carter follows after him, leaving me standing here with her as tremors rock her tiny body. God, she would be so easy to break.

"I'm rough and tend to break my toys, but I'll try to be gentle and not break you." She gasps but says nothing as I push her forward. She stumbles but I do nothing to help her. She places one foot in front of the other, heading toward the guys. She can hold her head high and try to keep her shoulders square, but we all know she is freaking the fuck out and trying to act tough. God, if she was really into this shit, then she would be the perfect girl for the three of us.

One night with her should help our cravings. Yes, we all fuck each other and get off but nothing compares to the warmth of a wet pussy wrapped around your cock as you slam inside it. The sounds a woman makes is like none other and I know for a fact Karley Le Roux will be just as perfect as I have pictured her to be.

She may not know us but we know her.

"On the table," Vaughn barks. She takes a step forward and grips the edge of the table but Carter tsks, halting her movements. She lifts her gaze to him and quirks a brow.

"I'm doing as he said!" she snaps.

"Lose the clothes, beauty." Her jaw unhinges as she stares at him. "It's not a request," he adds when she doesn't move quick enough for his liking. She darts her gaze to Vaughn who just crosses his arms over his chest. She peers over at me, I shove my hands in my pockets showing her without words she's on her own. "You get a choice, either play with us or brave your chances out there with the real crazy ones and see how well you fare considering they haven't seen a woman in *years*."

His warning hangs heavy in the air. She weighs her options for a second, then shakily grips the hem of her shirt and slowly pulls it over her head. The black bra she wears does little to hold her full tits in place. Apprehension is clear in her posture when she reaches for the button on her pants. If she expects any of us to grow a conscience and stop her, she is out of her fucking mind. I would rather lick Carter's asshole than stop this.

The air charges with need when she pushes her

pants down her legs and kicks them to the side. She refuses to remove her shoes, showing us her defiance. The sight of her in her black bra and matching boy shorts that show off the underside of her ass cheeks has my cock straining against my pants, begging to be set free, so I can slam inside her and feel the warmth of her pussy encasing me like a glove.

"Fuck, I bet you're tight as fuck, aren't you?" Vaughn's voice is filled with unfiltered need. She ignores his question as she grips the edge of the table and hoists herself up. She sits there with her legs dangling over the edge for a moment and closes her eyes taking a deep breath.

"Fuck it," she mutters, then maneuvers herself so she is laying down. A hiss escapes her luscious lips when the cold metal touches her skin. It's clear Vaughn wants to ravage her like an animal—none of us expected her to look like she does. We had expected her to come in here with a holier than thou attitude and think her shit doesn't stink, but she is blowing our fucking minds right now.

She wraps her fingers around the edge of the slab in a vice-like hold, her chest rising and falling rapidly, the anticipation riding her hard.

"Tonight, we're going to give you all that you need but not what you want," Carter says.

She tips her head to the side and stares at him for a long moment. "I don't know what the hell that means."

"It means we're going to take turns making you come but never put our cocks inside you because you haven't earned the right to feel them inside you," I answer for him. She jerks her head back my way and stares at me with a deer-caught-in-the-headlights look in her eyes. I smirk behind my mask, she may not say the words but this dirty little slut was hoping we would fuck her nine ways to hell and make her forget her own damn name.

Her jaw pops open. I reach out and push her mouth shut. "Next time she opens that mouth, I'm shoving my cock in it," Carter growls. I feel her jaw tighten and groan. I just know breaking her is going to be so much fun. Vaughn moves so he is at the end of the table. He hits the switch on the side of the tray that kills all the lights in the room and turns the one directly above her on, blinding her from seeing anything. Her eyes slam closed instantly to ward off the burn from the sudden assault on her retinas.

Carter and I grip her wrists while Vaughn secures her ankles in the straps. She tries to fight but it's pointless. "What the fuck are you doing?" she yells.

"When you beg for it to stop, we won't. You're restrained for *our* safety, not yours," Vaughn growls in a tone filled with pure lust. At his admission she quits fighting but doesn't relax. Carter and I make quick work of securing her wrists. The flush that rolls through her creamy skin once she is secured tells us she loves this shit.

Carter and I move to join Vaughn. I push him out of the way, needing to be the first to taste her. I remove my mask and place it on the small trolley beside the slab. I trail my fingers up her legs, loving the shiver that rolls through her at my touch. The moment I reach the apex of her thighs she sucks in a sharp breath.

I glide my index finger down the front of her panties and growl my approval when I feel how wet she is. "You soaked through your panties, you nasty little bitch." My words have her trembling but she keeps her mouth shut, causing Carter to chuckle.

"He's going to eat your pussy while my friend fucks him. When he makes you come, we'll switch and I'll get to fuck him while he makes you come again. We're going to keep doing this until you pass the fuck out and can't even remember where you are." Vaughn's decree has her gasping.

"If you're a good girl and play the game well, we

might even let you play with our cocks tomorrow night," Carter adds.

"We'll make sure you're ready to take all three of us at once. When the doors open tomorrow and you run, we'll chase you, little psycho, and when we catch you, you will learn why we are devils," I vow.

I have no time to process their words. He pushes my panties to the side and hums his approval at the mess of my arousal between my legs. I may not be able to see a damn thing but my hearing is heightened and fuck, something about not being able to see what is happening only adds to my growing need. When he blows on my sensitive pussy I whimper, I'm so sensitive from all the edging and the fact they had no idea that everything they have done tonight has only served to enhance my carnal desires.

If there was ever a way to say *fuck you* to my dad for putting me in here, this is it.

My train of thought is derailed when he swipes his tongue through my folds, my back arching off the metal slab as I cry out. He grips the sides of my thighs in a punishing hold as he buries his face in my pussy. I scream so loud the sound echoes through the room. I'm jolted forward and gasp when I hear a grunt.

Are they really going to fuck each other while one of them eats me out?

My question is answered when moans begin to fill the room. Pheromones tinge the air as my need begins to grow to new heights. I fucking hate the light above me, I would give anything to watch the three of them fuck. Jesus, that is one of my bucket list items and it's happening right in front of me but I can't see it!

I want to riot over the fact that a fantasy of mine has finally come to light but the feeling of his tongue pressing against me, and the sensations he is creating without my consent, forces my mind to focus on the feeling, not what is happening around me as every swipe of his tongue brings me nearer to the edge. His fingers pressed into the soft flesh of my skin as he forces his tongue inside my tight, wet little hole.

"You like getting your dirty little pussy eaten while we take turns fucking each other?"

"I want to watch as you fuck each other." I don't care that I'm begging. I don't care that they're strangers. All I care about is my need to come and I want them to do it with me. Just as I feel my orgasm rising, the one eating my pussy grunts and then stops. I want to moan and shout when he pulls back, but then his face is quickly replaced by another and fuck me does he know what he is doing. With every swipe of his tongue, he pushes me closer to the edge and the second he buries two fingers inside my tight little cunt and one in my ass, I detonate all over his face.

I come so hard, screaming loud enough to wake the dead.

I don't get a chance to come down from my high before one of them groans their release and then the face between my legs is replaced by another. His rough stubble scraps against my sensitive skin, pulling a gasp from me. Tremors still roll through me in waves. The moment he sucks my clit into his mouth I cry out. I'm still so sensitive and need a minute to come down but they won't allow it, even when I beg.

The next orgasm tears through me with the grace of a tornado and shreds me apart. I can hear them fucking and it grates on my fucking nerves that I can't see it.

"Please, no more," I plead, but my pleas fall of

deaf ears. My only reprieve from the glorious torture is when they switch with each other and those few seconds feel like I am finally able to breathe again. After the fifth orgasm, tears stream down my face. My body is wrung out and my mind is reeling with a thousand thoughts but also blank at the same time. I can't focus, I can barely remember to breathe and I'm fighting to stay conscious.

Women think their body can handle multiple orgasms but they're dead fucking wrong.

How do I know? Because I was one of those fucking women who prayed they would find a man whose sole purpose was to make them come repeatedly and now that I finally have my wish come true, I don't want it.

When I feel another orgasm cresting I begin to thrash against my restraints and fight for my freedom. "Pass out or forget your name, those are the rules," one of them says, the satisfaction in his tone mocking and annoyance chills against my sensitive skin like a rash. I want to punch the smug expression from his face and render him speechless.

"Fuck you. I quit. I don't want to play anymore," I scream and try to pull on the restraints again, but it's useless. I never should have allowed this to happen but yet again, I couldn't back down from a challenge and that is the reason my father no doubt sent me here, to teach me a lesson. I never can shut my mouth and just walk away.

"If you quit, there is a punishment you must face," one of the others says. I'm ready to tell them to kiss my ass and go to hell but when my next orgasm tears through me, I break. My mind turns blank, my body goes numb as the release slams into me. My mouth opens but no sound escapes as I'm forced to ride out the wave of pleasure that they are inflicting on me. Blood pumps in my ears, muting all the sounds around me. When I feel my consciousness fleeing I don't fight it, I embrace it and allow the darkness to consume and save me from having to admit defeat against these three masked fucks.

I wake slowly and sit up while still keeping my eyes closed, only to smack my head on something. I flop back down and groan. When I reach up to rub my forehead my hand smacks something, causing me to open my eyes only to see nothing but darkness. Dread begins to set in. I snap my arms out and feel around—all I can feel is ice-cold metal. When I part my legs, I feel the same thing. I try to shimmy downward only to be met with a wall. I stretch my arms above my head and feel the same thing.

Full on panic sets the fuck in and I start to feel claustrophobic.

"Breathe, Karley," I mutter to myself. "In and out. You're not trapped." No matter how many times I repeat that line over and over I can't force myself to believe it. It's pitch black and I can't see a damn thing. Tears trek down my cheeks without permission. I'm not the type of girl that cries or gets on social media and posts selfies, I'm the live in the moment type, and right now I can't find the badass bitch that I am daily inside me anywhere. "Help!" I scream as I begin to kick and pound my fists against the walls of this metal box I am trapped inside of. "Please help me!" Sobs claw their way out of me as my movements turn frantic with the need to escape. My chest tightens and breathing becomes a chore, I can't get enough air into my lungs and I start to hyperventilate.

I scream for so long and so loud my throat grows hoarse, full on sobs wrack my body and exhaustion weighs on me. I'm cold and shivering. Whimpers continue to escape me as I lay here utterly at the mercy of the men who trapped me in here.

Those masked freaks better hope I die in here. If I make it out of this hell I'll ruin each of those bastards, starting with ripping their cocks off.

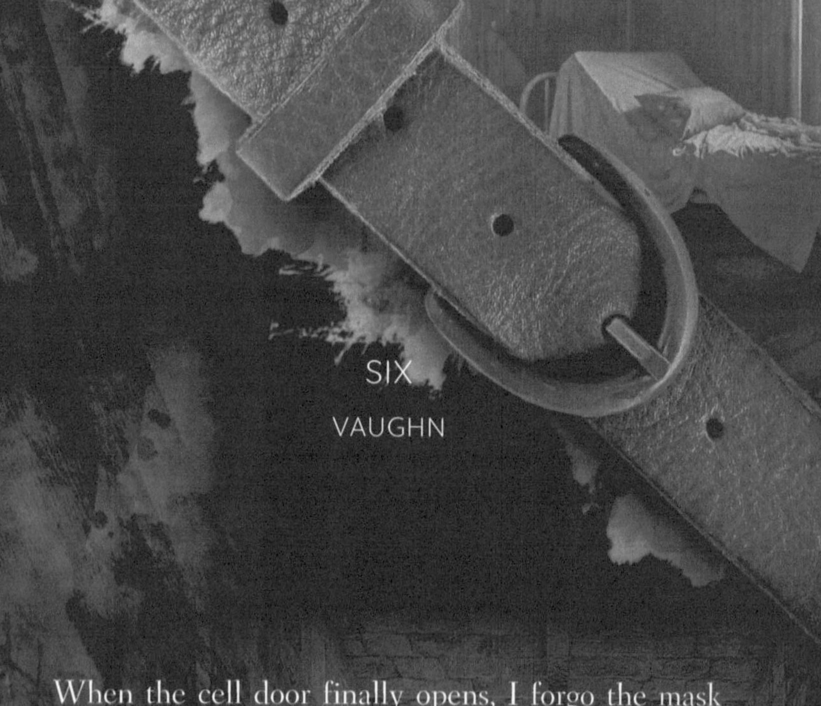

When the cell door finally opens, I forgo the mask like we had planned and stalk down the hallway with Carter at my side, ignoring the stares of the others. I push the door open that will lead us down to the morgue, where we housed our guest to keep her safe from the others. I don't relish the idea of these fuckers touching our new toy and all of them were made aware this morning that the girl some may have seen running last night is off limits. If they dare to break our decree, they know they will pay with their lives.

We own Slade Le Roux.

This is our kingdom and though we may hate being trapped here, we make the best of this fucked-up situation. Soon, we will be free of this place.

"Draven not coming?" Carter asks as he opens the door.

"No. She knows his face and it would be better for the two of us to do this without him. He'd give into his demons the moment he sees her." Draven is a predator, so once he sets his sights on something he wants there is no stopping him. Karley Le Roux is his prey and it will only be a matter of time before he finally snaps and makes his move to claim her, we need to finish this before Draven can complete his hunt.

"He's gonna be pissed."

I shrug as I follow him down the stairs. "I made sure his cell door would remain locked long enough for us to do what we needed to."

Carter whistles. "He's gonna be on a rampage tomorrow."

I nod even though he can't see me. "I know. Tomorrow, we'll give him the girl to curb his urges and keep him distracted so he doesn't kill us." Carter laughs. Draven is our brother. The three of us were forced together and through that we forged an unbreakable bond. Carter and Draven are the only reason I haven't lost my mind while being locked in this fucking hell. The moment we enter the morgue her quiet cries can be heard. Carter turns to face me and smiles.

I nod to him and both of us plaster on looks of concern as we make our way to her chamber. I pull the door open as Carter grips the slab and pulls it out. The instant she is free she sits up and strikes out too fast for me to dodge her punch. The bitch lands a right hook to my cheek. She tries to lurch off the slab but Carter wraps an arm around her waist and holds her in place.

"Let me go!" she screams. I glare at the little shit and rub my cheek. It takes her a second to take in my appearance and the clothing I wear. When she looks over her shoulder at Carter and takes in his maskless face and the button-down shirt he wears, her face slackens. "You work here?" she rasps out.

"Yes," Carter and I answer in unison.

The tension drains out of her body and she slouches in his hold. "Thank God, you have to help me. I was locked in there by some masked freaks—"

"Shhhh, calm down," Carter coos as I move across the room and retrieve some scrubs from one of the lockers. I place them on the slab beside her and turn my back to offer her the illusion of privacy when in truth, I've tasted that sweet pussy and hunger for another chance to bury my tongue inside that tight little cunt. Fuck, she responded to the three of us so well last night, she lasted longer than I thought she would. Carter comes to stand beside me, keeping his back to her while she dresses.

"Who are you?" she asks after a couple minutes. Carter and I slowly turn and face her. The scrubs are too big for her and swallow her tiny body, but the deranged look in her eyes and the way her hair is wild and untamed only fuels the beast inside me that hungers for the chance to bury my cock inside her and mark her as mine.

"I'm Carter, I'm the chaplain here and this is my associate, Vaughn, the resident therapist." She darts her gaze between the two of us with clear judgment in those green eyes that has me wanting to wrap my hand around her throat.

"This place has a priest?"

Carter chuckles. "I'm not a priest, I'm just a chaplain. Now, how about we get you set up in your cell?" She jerks back and shakes her head.

"I am not going back up there with that fucking psycho!" she spits.

"Draven Bailey?" I press, her gaze cutting to me with a vicious look as she bares her teeth.

"Yes, that son of a bitch."

"His mother was actually a lovely lady. Tragic

that she died not long ago while her son was locked up in here." Her face slackens at my admission and remorse is plastered across her face.

"Condolences and all that, but that bastard set me up last night and him and his masked freaks locked me in that fucking thing after..." She clamps her mouth closed, unable to finish.

"After, what?" I push, taking a step toward her, causing her eyes to widen slightly at my bold move. Her mouth parts but no words escape. "Hmmm, I think it's a good idea for you to come with me." Without waiting for a reply I grip her arm and lead her out of there. She doesn't struggle but I notice how she looks back to make sure Carter is following. The fact she trusts him after mere minutes is a fool's move. Once we reach the top of the stairs she begins to pull back against my hold.

"I'm not going out there," she hisses.

I roll my eyes. "No one will harm you while you are with us," is all I say before I push the door open and drag her out. She tries to struggle against my hold but she's no match for me. All her resistance does is cause my cock to jerk to attention with the need to fuck the fight out of her. How she is related to that double crossing cunt is a mystery to me. She is no coward like her father, she is courageous enough to embrace her desires and relish in them.

The instant we step into the hall she stops fighting. Patients are scattered around, enjoying their freedom but the moment they see her, all their chatter stops. She presses against my back, keeping close as I walk down the corridor toward her cell. I make sure to give each of these fucks a look telling them she's off limits to everyone but us.

She fists the back of my shirt with her other hand, which has me fighting back a smile. She trusted Carter by instinct because he said he was a chaplain but now that we are up here and in view of the others, she is latching onto me because the girl is smart enough to know I call the fucking shots. The fact that all of them part to make way for us, only serves to prove I am the one with the power here and if she's smart, she will obey my every demand... Or, I might just have to punish her and allow her to think I would let these cunts touch what I have declared as mine already.

SEVEN

KARLEY

I have my face practically buried into the back of his shirt, I don't come out of my hiding place even when we have stopped moving. I don't know when he stopped dragging me by my arm and I began clinging to him, but the sight of all those vicious faces out there was enough to alert me to the fact that I was safer with these two rather than risking myself out there. I'm not thrilled at the idea of needing to have someone protect me, I'm used to relying on myself.

I may have a father but he was never around. I was raised by nannies and maids in a house the size of a castle. I was used to being alone and looking out for myself. So, being thrust into a place like this, where I have to rely on others for my safety, is going to be harder than swallowing fucking razor blades.

My dad is self-centered and loves his money more than anything or *anyone*.

"You're safe here," Carter says. I slowly release my hold on Vaughn and look around the room, trying to hide my apprehension at the sight of the concrete cell we stand in. There is a metal toilet with no seat in the corner and a rusted basin. A metal frame bed with a mattress thinner than a sanitary pad and a threadbare blanket that looks itchy as fuck, but the sight of the blood-stained pillow is what has my stomach rolling.

"Are these accommodations not up to your standards?" The mockery in Vaughn's voice is clear and I refuse to allow this asshole to get the upper hand, so I pull up my big girl panties and waltz across the room, sit on the edge of the bed and release a pleased sigh.

"Nope." I pop the 'P' just to piss him off. "This is perfect and will do just fine until I get out." Both of them snort and shake their heads which just irritates me. "I won't be here long."

Vaughn's face remains a mask of loathing while Carter at least has the decency to seem remorseful when he looks at me.

"Once you are admitted to Slade Le Roux, you never leave." His statement has my brows drawing together.

"Yeah, I think you have that wrong."

"Do I?" he volleys back.

With false bravado I meet his stare head on and nod. "Yes. Even inmates are released from prison."

When the both of them share a loaded look, a trickle of unease slides down my spine. "Enjoy the solitude while you have it, Miss Le Roux. These walls tend to close in on you and force you to embrace the darkest parts of yourself or you risk losing your sanity completely," Carter says ominously.

"You'll be here a long time, so I suggest you start dealing with the demons of your past before they *chase* you down," Vaughn growls, then stalks out of the cell. Carter shoots me one last look before following after his friend. If they are the chaplain and the resident therapist, then I'm fucked. Neither of them looked like they actually wanted to help me, if anything it looked like they were happy I was in here with them and these bunch of unhinged motherfuckers.

I've been sitting in the same spot for so long my back has grown stiff from sitting upright without moving. When I hear a faint scuff I gingerly climb to my feet, I freeze in fear at the sight of a crowd of men just outside my doorway. It never dawned on me that

I should have closed the cell door or asked Vaughn and Carter if they could lock me in here. When the skinhead smiles wide and gives me a full view of his yellow teeth, I cringe and step back.

My show of distress at his intimidation only seems to fuel his interest. He takes a bold step forward and now stands in the cell with me. I have no weapons to defend myself with. I'm scrappy but I'm no fucking MMA fighter!

"Look what we got ourselves here, boys," he taunts, the crowd behind him cheering him on like a flock of fucking sheep. "I reckon she could take us."

"Fuck. You." I grit each word out slowly. The bastard's eyes narrow and it's then that I see the true crazy in his eyes. This place was built to house those too clinically out of their mind for prison. The men locked in here are a true risk to society and now I have found myself backed into a corner with a hoard of them waiting for their pound of flesh.

The fucker launches at me and I throw hands like I'm Mike Tyson's granddaughter. I scratch, punch and claw the bastard, but when his fist connects with my cheek, I drop to the ground like a sack of potatoes. My vision is fuzzy, but when I hear him roar in pain, I shake my head to clear my dazed eyesight. A part of me wishes I hadn't, but another part can't stop watching as the purple devil with the snapped horns from last night straddles him and grips his head between his hands, then begins smashing it against the concrete ground with such force I cringe when I hear his head crack.

I open my mouth to tell him to stop or he will kill him but words fail me. I snap my head to the side when I hear the crowd begin to whimper in fear. One of the guys shoots me a sorrowful look before he pushes the door closed, locking me in here with the masked killer. I flinch when I hear another crack and slowly turn back to face them, only to have to swallow back the bile rushing up my throat at the sight of the guy's head caved in and blood flowing along the ground toward me. I shuffle backward on my ass to escape being touched by the blood, but the cell is so small I hit the wall.

At the sound of my grunt, he whips his head toward me and I gulp. His brown eyes burn with rage and I start trembling. Last night he and his buddies had their faces buried between my legs and now this one is looking at me like I'm his next meal— not in a good way. I cringe when he releases the guy's head and I see the blood covering his hands and clothing. He wears the same blue scrubs as I do, granted there isn't much blue left visible on his now.

"Scared?" he taunts. I draw my knees up to my chest when the trail of blood comes closer. I stare at it, willing it to stop but of course it doesn't and the second it comes into contact with my pants it spreads like wildfire. I bite back my whimper and close my eyes, praying that the next time I open them, this will all be a bad dream and I'll wake up in my bed back home. When I finally open my eyes after a moment, I shriek at the sight of the masked devil crouching down in front of me.

Before I can move or utter a single word his blood covered hands cup my face between them. "They locked me in my room tonight." My eyes slant together. "They wanted you for themselves, my psycho, but I got out." I shake my head and open my mouth but he shifts his hand and places his bloody index finger over my lips and shushes me. "It's okay, tonight I get you all to myself and I plan to make you black out again, but this time when you pass out, it will be with my cock inside you and the coppery taste of his blood on your lips." My eyes snap wide.

"Are you fucking kidding me?" I snap. "You just killed a man and you expect me to fuck you next to his corpse?" When he tilts his head side to side I balk. "You're out of your fucking mind—"

"Yes. But I'm still going to fuck you in his blood

so every motherfucker in this hellhole will know what happens when they try and play with my toy."

"I'm not a fucking toy, you freak!" I scream.

His mocking laughter just grates on my nerves. "I plan to show you just how much of a freak I am and you will love every *inch* of it." Before I can register what the fuck is happening, he retrieves something that looks like a remote from his pants pocket, then pushes a button and I hear the distinct sound of my door locking. Then he presses another and the room is bathed in darkness. I open my mouth to scream for help but the sound is cut out when he lifts his mask enough to expose his mouth, smashes his lips on mine and swallows my screams.

EIGHT

DRAVEN

Fuck!

Tonight started off bad. When I realized those fuckers locked me in my room I went apeshit. I was prepared to spend the night plotting out how I was going to make them grovel, but then I remembered the three of us have master remotes. When I stepped foot out of my room and saw a crowd gathered around the room opposite mine—Carter and Vaughn's room—I knew she was in there. When I saw Benny lay his hands on her, I saw red. Killing isn't anything new to me but the look of fear in her eyes when she looked at me, I hated it.

I had to erase that look and judging from the way her arms wrap around my neck, and how she is pulling me against her, I would say I have done a stellar job of distracting her from the body lying beside us. I'm so hard just thinking about her covered in blood, and being able to fuck her next to a corpse is going to bring a dream of mine to life.

I'm not a necrophiliac, but fucking next to the dead *is* something I'm into.

I push against her until she is flat on her back on the floor, Benny's blood pooling around her. I break the kiss and look down at her with blood forming a halo of sorts and that sight alone has me rock fucking hard and my cock threatening to tear through my pants. She opens her mouth to no doubt argue, but I silence her when I push her shirt up and expose that taunting bra from last night that was begging me to bite her tits. She keeps staring at my mask, wondering who the fuck I am but she will never know it's me. Vaughan, Carter and I always switch masks to keep everyone guessing.

I yank the cups of her bra down and expose her tits. They aren't huge, but they are the perfect size to fit in my hands and that's exactly what I do. She whimpers at the feeling of my touch, but seeing the blood from my hands on her creamy skin has me groaning and wanting to lick her clean.

"Take the mask off," she pants out.

I smirk down at the little psycho. "You need to earn that and so far you have earned nothing but my cock." Her face slackens but her eyes pulse with need. This girl is an anomaly and gets off on all the same sick shit as I do. Without being prompted, I lean down and suck one of her nipples into my mouth and relish the sound of her scream reverberating off the walls.

I bite down, groaning when she cries out in pain but doesn't beg me to stop. I switch sides and do the same thing but when I bite down, this time she doesn't cry out in pain, she moans in pleasure. I release her nipple making sure to scrape my teeth along it, loving the whimper that escapes.

I rest back on my haunches and secure my mask in place. Her mouth parts but I silence her when I grip the crotch of her pants and shred it, exposing her panties. Without hesitation, I push the material to the side and growl at the sight of her perfect pink pussy, dripping wet for me.

"You putrid slut, look at the mess you've made."

"Please..."

I flick my gaze up to her. "*Please,* what?"

"Touch me," she begs.

Fuck, hearing her beg while covered in the blood of another has my restraint snapping. I push my pants down and expose my hard cock. Her eyes widen at the sight of it. I grip my dick in my hand and hiss at the feeling when I pump myself twice.

"You want this?"

"Yes!" she shouts as she squirms beneath me.

"Beg."

Her eyes widen more in surprise. "What?"

"Beg me to fuck your wretched cunt and I might consider it."

Defiance shines in those alluring eyes of hers, so to prompt her I release my cock and trail a finger through her soaking folds.

"Fuck!" she screams.

"Beg!" I snarl as I push a single finger inside her—fuck she's so tight. Her pussy clamps down on my finger, trying to hold me captive as I push in and out of her.

"Oh shit," she pants out when I press the pad of my thumb against her clit. I keep my pace steady and she chases her release, but when I feel the walls of her cunt clamp down on me, I withdraw my finger and smirk behind my mask at the sight of outrage plastered across her face. "What the fuck?"

"Beg, you filthy slut."

Her jaw locks and I pray she defies me so I can punish her. Unable to control myself as need erupts like a blazing fire inside me, I reach down and grip her hair, then use it to yank her to her feet, ignoring her cry of pain. I yank the sheet off the bed and drop it on the ground, before facing her and shredding her clothes with my bare hands. She stands there silent and stunned. I lean forward and unclasp her bra, her jaw unhinging when I drop to my knees and peel her panties down her legs. I rise and stand here for a second, taking in the sight of her bare and ready for the taking.

"Get on the bed." Without a sarcastic remark, she does as I say and lays down. I grab the sheet from the floor and shred it into strips, then use them to secure each of her wrists and ankles to the bed frame. Once I've finished, I look down at her and the sight of uncertainty in her eyes has me saying, "Say *stop* and I will."

She inhales sharply as her eyes shine with gratitude. "Don't stop," she whispers. I make quick work of losing my pants, then carefully remove my shirt so I don't dislodge my mask. She gapes at the sight of my cock standing proudly against my abs.

"I don't do soft, you take what the fuck I give and

say thank you when I'm done, got it?" She nods vigorously. "Say the fucking words, whore."

"Yes." Her acceptance is all I need. I climb on top of her and nestle between her legs. The way she keeps her eyes on me the whole time is fucking addictive, she isn't shy and doesn't cower away from her wants. I line my cock up and slowly push forward, stretching her tight little cunt to accommodate me. "Yes, fuck, yes," she chants as I continue to push inside her. When I bottom out, we both moan in unison.

"Fuck, this pussy is so fucking tight," I praise as I draw back and slam inside her hard. She cries out and the sound does nothing but fuel my savage need to claim her and mark her as mine. I reach down and slap her tits as I thrust inside her again.

"Holy shit, you feel fucking incredible," she moans. I see it in her eyes that she's getting frustrated with my slow thrusts, she wants me to fuck her hard and fast but I won't do that until she fucking begs me.

"This pussy belongs to me," I snarl.

"Yes."

"You only open these legs for me and my brothers." Her eyes widen in surprise.

"What?" I silence her by increasing my pace

slightly, bringing her to the edge only to stop. Orgasm denial is fucking brutal, but it's the best form of torture and watching her grow increasingly frustrated each time she feels her orgasm only to have it fade, is far too enthralling for me to give in and grant her what she wants.

NINE

CARTER

"What's the plan?" I ask Vaughn as I pace our cell, leaving her in that room alone wasn't my idea. Vaughn was waiting for her to cave and call us back and beg for protection but the little bitch is too stub-born. We've been in here for the past fifteen minutes waiting until the time was right to go back.

"Fuck, she is hot." Both Vaughn and I snap our heads toward the open door to see some guys walking past. I turn to my brother to find his gaze on me, without being prompted we both begin changing our clothes, pulling on our black pants and hoodie, then securing our masks. Unlike Draven, who prefers to stay on his own, Vaughn and I share a cell as it makes it easier during the day when we want to fuck, but Draven doesn't see it that way. He hates having people in his space so when we all fuck, he comes here.

Vaughn and I rush from the room and when we come to a stop outside her room, I try to pull the door open but it doesn't budge. "It's locked."

Vaughn pushes me aside and peers through the small glass window at the top of the door, then curses beneath his breath. "Fucking Draven!" he snarls, then retrieves the remote from his pocket and unlocks the door. The second he pushes it open all I hear is the sound of her cries. We enter the room, pulling the door closed behind us to see Draven fucking her on the bed while Benny's lifeless body lays on the floor. Both Draven and Karley are covered in blood and the sight is a fucking masterpiece.

She shrieks in surprise when she spots me and Vaughn standing here in our masks. She tugs against her restraints but they don't give. Draven just laughs and continues to fuck her.

"Stop!" she snaps. Drave pauses and looks down at her, his body coiled tight with anger.

"No. You want this and think stopping it will get you out of this situation but it won't. You want them to watch as I fuck you because you're a dirty cunt who wants them to take turns on you when I pull out." Her face slackens at his taunt, her mouth parts but no words come out. "Keep your eyes on them while I fuck you so they know it was my cock that got to break in this pussy before they did." A gasp escapes her but it's quickly turned into moans when Draven begins moving inside her again.

Watching him fuck her while she stares at us has my cock twitching in my pants. Her eyes widen in intrigue when I push my pants down and expose my cock. Her tongue darts out to moisten her lips and I smirk. I step forward and crouch down until my cock is in line with her face.

"Suck it," I snap. Her mouth pops open like a good little slut. I thrust forward viciously, causing her to gag but the sound doesn't deter me, it just fuels the beast inside me that craves those sounds, so I continue to fuck her face ruthlessly while I spy Vaughn out of the corner of my eye, stopping at the end of the bed behind Draven. He's naked sans his mask.

"Suck it hard," I bark as I watch Vaughn spit in his hand and begin lathering his dick, then pushes Draven forward so he is flat against Karley. When he parts Draven's ass and spits on his asshole I groan, it fucking gets me off watching them fuck. It's going to be a tight fit for them but I know Vaughn will make it work. I reach down and stroke her cheek, drawing her gaze to mine. I ease out of her mouth and smile behind my mask at the sight of her gasping for air. "Watch him slide his cock inside his ass, my brothers are both going to fuck you while you suck my dick."

"Oh sweet baby fucking Jesus," she pants out. She sits up as much as she can and watches as Vaughn climbs on the bed behind Draven, lines his dick up and pushes inside him. Draven groans at the feeling. A flush overrides her body as her need pulses to life at the sight of my brothers.

Vaughn growls when he thrusts forward and impales Draven on his cock, causing the latter to groan. Vaughn reaches out and grips Draven's shoulder for leverage so he can fuck him hard.

"Has she come?" I ask.

"No, he won't let me," she snaps. I smirk, knowing that she has zero chance in hell of coming tonight, Draven won't allow it. He'll leave her on edge for a while and maybe if she's lucky he'll put her out of her misery tomorrow night. "Please I need to—" I cut off her plea by burying my cock in her big mouth. She chokes on me and unwillingly swallows me down her throat, causing her to gag and thrash to get free.

"Breathe through your nose because I'm not

above getting head off a dead bitch," I hiss. Tears roll down her cheeks and all that sight does is fuel my need.

"Fucking take my dick, you cunt," Vaughn shouts as he slams inside Draven over and over again at a punishing pace. Karley tries to catch them off guard and ride Draven so she can come, but Vaughn knows Draven too well and knows he wouldn't have let her come, so each time she gets close he'll stop and wait a minute until the possibility of her orgasm passes before continuing.

Tears flow down her cheeks for an entirely different reason now, she's so wrung out and frustrated from not being able to come that she is short circuiting and the only thing she can focus on is her arousal. It's cruel as fuck to continue denying her, but this is not about her pleasure. She is a tool for us to use and exploit, not to care for and cherish. She is our ticket to freedom and being able to fuck her at the same time is a bonus, but the real reward is scaring the shit out of her and showing her the lengths we are willing to go to without exposing our true identity— it is the perfect revenge against *him*.

"Fuck, I'm gonna come down her throat," I grit out as I keep fucking her face like an animal. To her credit, she doesn't skip a beat or alter her movements.

she just opens her mouth wider allowing me better access. "Good girl."

"I'm gonna fill this ass up, then you're going to make her suck it out, got it?" Vaughn snaps. Draven groans and nods. His words send me hurtling over the edge, coming with a roar so loud it could wake Benny's lifeless ass. Karley guzzles every fucking drop of my release before I finally pull out of her mouth. She turns to look up at Draven and licks her lips, enticing him to taste her. The fucker one ups her by pulling out of her, drawing a cry of injustice from the girl as she is forced to lay there and watch as Vaughn fucks Draven. "Fuck!" Vaughn yells as he comes deep in Draven's ass. He doesn't wait for the aftershocks of his release to subside before he is pulling out of our brother and giving him room to move. Draven spins around and scoots up the bed on his knees until his ass is on her face. He pulls his cheeks open for her as he says,

"Suck his fucking cum out of me." I wait for her to protest and scream about how disgusting he is, but to all our surprise she just moans and does exactly as he says. Draven throws his head back, groaning when she begins licking his ass and making sure she's gotten every drop of Vaughn's cum out of him while he keeps stroking himself.

"Keep eating my ass. I'm about to cum all over this pussy," he snarls. Karley does as he says and not a minute later Draven comes with a roar so primal that Simba would be fucking proud. Jets of cum land on her stomach and the top of her pussy, branding her as our toy.

Karley Le Roux has no idea she now belongs to us and we plan to use her every single day until daddy dearest finally grants us our release from this hellhole he locked us in.

TEN

KARLEY

I'm so strung out and my frustration has only mounted as time ticks by. When they untied me and left me laying on the bed as they walked out and locked the door behind them, I thought it was some kind of joke but I was wrong. I'm left in this fucking cell with a dead body on the ground, it's head caved in and cum and blood crusted to my skin with no way of cleaning myself. All I have to cover my naked-ness and keep warm is one of the hoodies they left behind.

I've been huddled against the wall in the oppo-site corner from the body and bed for so long my body is aching and protesting. I'm too exhausted to move and terrified that the dead guy will wake up and try to eat me like *The Walking Dead*.

I've been fighting to stay awake but I keep dozing on and off. The last thing I want is for those masked freaks to come back and turn my body against me again for the third time. I don't know what it is with these assholes, but the whole mask thing and the fact they take what they want without remorse has me weak in the fucking knees. I need to focus on getting the fuck out of here, I need to find those two guys, Carter and Vaughn, and see if they can help me.

My stomach is cramping and making its hunger known but it's my throat that is the worst—the thirst is real. There is a basin in the corner but the sight of the rusty tap puts me off drinking from it.

I startle awake to the sound of the buzzer and the lock on the door clicking open. When my door opens on its own, I begin to tremble with worry that I may be attacked again or the masked fuckers will come back.

The least those bastards could do is get me off this time!

When three men enter the cell, I press my back harder against the wall, waiting for them to strike out but none of them look at me. Instead, they head straight for the body. Two of them grab an arm each while the third guy grabs both the legs on his own and they carry him out of here without even giving me a single glance. I sit here with bated breath just waiting for them to come back in and pick up where their friend left off yesterday. My eyes begin to burn from not blinking due to me staring at the open doorway for so long. Men walk past my cell but none of them even acknowledge me. Can they not see me?

A shriek of surprise lodges in my throat when Carter appears in the doorway. His features are pulled taut as he takes in the sight of me. I mull over what to say and try to come up with a way to explain the dried blood on the floor, bed and covering me but I doubt he would even believe me—it's not like I can tell the truth.

Hey, Carter. Some guy wearing a mask came in after you guys left, killed some asshole who tried to rape me, then fucked me in his blood. Oh, wait, his two other friends came in halfway through and decided to fuck my face and his ass while he fucked me.

I mentally snort, yeah, I need to come up with a good lie or this guy is going to lock me away in a padded room and toss the fucking key.

"Come with me." I learned my lesson last night about staying here alone so I follow him without complaint. I keep my head down and don't make eye contact with anyone as I pass by. After what seems like a million turns and a hundred hallways, he pushes open a door and motions for me to enter. I eye him warily for a moment before stepping inside…

"A bathroom," I breathe out.

"It's only used by the female staff. I managed to find some womanly products and placed them in the stall with a towel and change of clothes. I'll wait out here." I don't get a chance to reply or thank him before he closes the door and leaves me alone to wash away the blood and… semen coating my skin. Call me fucking stupid if you like, but as I strip off the hoodie and stand under the spray of water, I feel remorseful. Even when I brush my teeth I loathe that the taste of him is no longer on my tongue.

Once I'm finished, I step out and dry off. The clothes laid out for me are plain, white cotton bra and panties, gray sweats and plain white cotton long-sleeve shirt. A pair of socks and sneakers in my size rest on the ground. I don't dwell on the fact that Carter knows my clothing size or shoe size as I quickly change, then head out to meet him in the hallway. He looks me over, then nods and motions for me to follow after him.

This time, I do look around and take in my surroundings. The men that mill about the halls look malnourished and filthy, their clothes torn and look like they haven't been washed in months. A couple of the guys walk with a limp and look as if they are in pain. Unable to keep my mouth closed any longer, I ask Carter.

"Are any of the patients here getting medication or access to clean clothing?" Carter slams to a stop and whirls around to face me, the look of surprise on his face renders me silent.

He scans my face searching for something but I'm not sure what. "Do you actually care?" His tone is firm and has me narrowing my eyes.

"I wouldn't ask if I didn't!" I hiss.

"Why would you care about these people?" The accusation in his tone grates on my nerves.

"Because I do. Even murderers are entitled to clean living accommodations and medicine. This place is fucking horrendous and horrible. No one should have to live like this." I mutter the last part as I look at an elderly man across the hall from me, he's gripping his side, coughing, and it sounds painful.

"The owner of this place doesn't care. He gets paid to keep everyone here, not to keep them healthy, clothed and fed."

Shame washes over me. The owner of this place is my father and I have no doubt if any of these men found out I would be as good as dead.

"Do me a favor, when the devils come to you, do as they say because they own this place and they are the only ones who can keep you alive in here." My jaw slackens as Carter turns and walks away. It takes me a second to compose myself before I am chasing after him.

Carter leads me into a food hall and instructs me to wait by a table while he gathers me food and water. I thought we would stay in the crowded room but he leads me back to my *room*—I use that word loosely because I refuse to admit I am sleeping in a cell.

When Carter hands me the tray of food and water, I practically inhale the food and down the water a few gulps.

"I'll leave you to it. You have an hour before the devils will come knocking." I choke and splutter on my water as I stare up at Carter, the knowing look in his eyes has me cringing. "Cameras are fitted throughout this place... even the morgue," he says cockily, then shoots me a wink and walks out like he didn't just blow my fucking mind.

ELEVEN

VAUGHN

Hearing from Carter that she was concerned for one of the old guys in here almost had me questioning myself. Except, I know Robert Le Roux, and that motherfucker doesn't have a kind bone in his body. I know he would have raised his bitch of a daughter to be exactly like him. She's a good actress, I give her that. She's an even better lay and bitch can take dick better than a hooker looking for her next fix.

"Ready?" I pull my mask down and nod at Draven. He and Carter stalk out of my office and go in search of Karley. She has her first therapy appointment with me tomorrow and I'm almost gleeful at being able to get a chance to see inside her mind and find out what makes her tick, so I can use it against her and have more leverage against her father.

The three of us move in sync. The inmates may know our faces and know who we are beneath the masks, but even these sick fucks can register the difference between when we wear the masks and when we don't. The masks mean we are hunting and ready to fuck shit up, without the masks we play our roles.

"What the fuck is going on?" Carter hisses beneath his breath. A crowd has gathered in the middle of the hall and that shit is never a good sign, it means one of these fuckers has broken our rules and we are required to dish out punishment. As we push our way through the crowd, my excitement over the prospect of being able to break bones vanishes when I see Karley on the ground with one of the oldest guys in here, resting his head in her lap. He's pale and looks short of breath. Frank has been in here for over twenty years now. He was a banker who refused to grant Robert a loan and that bastard had him committed here.

The old timer was diagnosed with cancer four years ago, and in this place you don't get chemo let alone any type of medical attention. I strain my hearing to hear what Karley is saying to him.

"...It's okay, I'll stay with you until... It's... time. I

won't let you be alone. You have my word." My face pulls taut at her empty promise. The moment he starts coughing blood, that wannabe princess is going to run for the fucking hills. God forbid she messes up her hundred-dollar manicure.

"P-please f-f-find my..." Frank begins coughing and wheezing, you can hear in his tone it's taking all his strength to get the words out.

"I swear, I'll find your wife and tell her." The sight of tears rolling down her cheeks has me snapping. I push the remainder of the way forward, breaking through the crowd until she notices me standing here in Carter's mask. I expect to see surprise or fear on her face but all I see is anger. "You can fuck right off. I made a promise and I'm not leaving him!" she snarls. When Carter and Draven come to stand beside me, wearing their masks, panic flares in her eyes. She tries to conceal the look but fails. She knows we're the ones in control and if we were to drag her out of here by her fucking hair, no one would stop us. We've earned this respect and some little cunt like her isn't going to come into our home and think she can call the motherfucking shots.

We are the kings of this place and we kneel to no one!

I feel the eyes of everyone gathered around focused on us, waiting to see what our next move will be. Frank isn't the first person to die in this place and he sure as fuck won't be the last. Without uttering a single word, I push forward and bend down, ready to lift him, but she bands her arms around the old timer and clutches him against her. Her eyes burn with fierce protectiveness over the stranger.

"Please," she begs. "He doesn't have long left. I'll do whatever you want and take any punishment you feel like doling out but don't make me leave him."

"He won't take his last fucking breath inside the walls of this hellhole," I grit out through clenched teeth and pull him from her hold. She jumps to her feet and chases after me as I head for the back doors.

"Where are you taking him?" she screams. She grips my arm and tries to pull me to a stop but Carter rips her back by her ponytail.

"Shut the fuck up and follow," Draven hisses as Carter releases her and both my boys follow after me. Frank loves the outdoors and if his time is near then I know the old man would want to look at the night sky one last time. Karley follows us without uttering a word. Once we are outside, I stalk across the basketball court and head for the wooded area. Frank sighs in contentment.

"Thank... you," he rasps out as I gently place him on the ground. Karley pushes past Draven and drops to the ground beside Frank, fresh tears rolling down her cheeks. We all know he has mere minutes. "Don't... cry," he mutters.

She reaches out and cups his cheek in her small hand, the gesture has me and my boys all hyper focused on her.

"I'm so sorry you had to end up here. I wish I could change the outcome for you." The truth in her words rings out. All three of us share a loaded look. I know Carter wants to believe she is good but I can't. She shares that snake's DNA and is a product of his demonic ways. I see his face every time I look at her.

"The outcome would be the same, once you pass through the doors of this place you are forgotten. Frank won't be remembered after this night," Carter says ominously. He may sound like he's talking out of his ass but he isn't. There is no communication with the outside world in here. The three of us may be afforded extra privileges but we don't even have a way to make a single fucking phone call!

"Maybe for you but not for me. I will never forget him or this night." She dismisses us by focusing on Frank. She shifts so she is sitting behind him and has his head resting in her lap once again. His breathing has slowed.

It won't be long now.

Frank was one of the guys who helped me transition when I was locked in here. I may not be able to show emotion right now but he knows I care for him. I will be the one to prepare his body for its final resting place out back.

"I'll find her, Frank. I'll tell your Ellie how much you loved her and I promise to ease her worries and never mention how horrible this place was to you. I'll paint her a beautiful picture of a life well lived and never allow her to know the true horrors you endured." Her words put him at peace and allow him to finally let go and stop fighting. Frank takes one last shuddering breath, his eyes still fixed on the star-filled sky as he passes. Karley didn't even know him, yet she sobs for the man.

I don't do emotions, they are a weakness I can't afford.

"Take him," I snap, then turn and head back inside to prepare the morgue. Her screams of protest follow but the guys aren't deterred. They know we have a job to do and limited time to do it as there is no embalming or coffins in this place. We're lucky we even have two shovels to dig the fucking holes we put the bodies in. Frank's death just reconfirms every-thing we have done to get Karley here is the right move. Tonight she is going to learn the real reason she was brought here and what role she is to play in this.

TWELVE

KARLEY

The three of them refuse to allow me down into the morgue with them and instructed two men to escort me back to my cell, tasking them with making sure I didn't try to leave. I wanted to fight and scream but what good would it have done me? They don't care about my wants, all they want is to fuck me and use my body. I'm nothing but a fuck doll to them. I plan to use that to my advantage.

Waking up the next morning, I prepare myself for the long boring day ahead of being locked in this shithole cell. That idea is blown out the window when my door opens and I find Vaughn standing there.

"Your therapy session begins now." His tone is anything but kind and open.

He drags a chair in with him and places it directly across from where I sit on the edge of the bed. He folds his large body as he takes a seat. Vaughn is fucking imposing, but much like the guy I met the first night, he is fucking gorgeous. Unlike Carter who has that boy next door type of look, Vaughn is ruggedly handsome and has a dark aura that surrounds him.

"Aren't therapists supposed to be inviting and all smiles or some shit?" I press.

His features pull taut and his eyes narrow. "You are aware that you are in an insane asylum, right?"

The mockery in his tone is clear. I fight not to bristle and give him the satisfaction of knowing he is getting to me. I don't know what it is about Vaughn, but this asshole sets me on edge and has me wanting to push his buttons to get a rise out of him, like I do with my masked freaks.

"Really? I thought I was staying in the Hilton. I mean you couldn't tell by my lavish penthouse suite. But, the view is to die for—"

"Is that what you want?"

"What?"

"To die?" I reel back in shock.

I shake my head. "I never said that."

"You didn't need to."

"What the fuck are you getting at here?"

"I want to get inside your head and see what makes you tick. I want to see your greatest nightmares come to life. I want to know what gets you off, what makes your heart skip a beat. I want to know what it's like to be inside you." His statement renders me speechless. I may not be an expert but I also know he has crossed a fucking line here professionally.

"Get. Out." I force out through clenched teeth.

He leans back in his chair and crosses his arms over his chest, then shoots me a self-satisfied smirk. "Getting under your skin, am I, Miss Le Roux?" Hearing my last name come out of his sinful mouth has the hairs on the back of my neck standing up. My breathing turns choppy, Vaughn will no doubt use my identity against me and after witnessing what happened to Frank last night, there is no doubt in my mind that every male in here would enjoy tearing me to fucking shreds.

"What do you want?"

"I just told you."

"No, you smug fuck. You're fucking with me and trying to blackmail me because you know my father is the one who owns this shithole. So again, what the fuck do you want?"

His whole demeanor shifts. He leans forward and rests his arms on the tops of his thighs, his face an inch from mine. I can smell his cool minty breath, his dark brown eyes almost appearing black. I see the devil inside him, lurking just beneath the surface. The urge to push him overrides my common sense. I lean in until our noses are touching, my bold move seeming to shock him, but he refuses to budge an inch not wanting me to get the upper hand.

"Keep pushing me, Vaughn, and you won't like the bitch I become."

"You're already a bitch, I'm just exposing your true identity."

"What the fuck are trying to play at here? What is your end game? I've seen no other staff here aside from you and Carter. Three masked freaks have the run of this place and answer to no one. Why is that?"

In a move so bold I don't see it coming, he snaps his arm, encircles my throat, then shoves me back on the bed and nestles himself between my legs. I stare up at Vaughn with wide eyes and my jaw slack.

"You listen to me, you little cunt." I gasp at his crass words. "You will do as I say because it is by my mercy that you have been unharmed in this place. Those masked freaks as you like to call them are your protection. So, if I were you, I would start showing some gratitude for their sacrifice. Your last name may grant you certain privileges and freedoms outside of these walls, but in here your last name will get you killed, so remember that."

An ungodly sound escapes me. I stare him right in the eyes and shudder at the look in them. Vaughn wants to see me hurt, he wants me in pain and I believe him now about wanting to see inside my head, but I just don't think he means that figuratively.

I throw my arms around his neck and pull him in closer so my lips ghost over his. If my move shocked him, he doesn't show it. "If you were going to kill me, you would have done it when you and Carter found me in the morgue. You need me alive for something and I plan to figure out what that reason is."

Vaughn growls but doesn't budge an inch, even when I skate my fingers through his hair. He's a master of disguising his face and I have a thing for trying to figure people out. I know without an ounce of a doubt, I'm going to be fixated on this man until I figure out what makes him tick. It's a flaw of mine but I can't help but want to fix people and find out what makes them *them*.

His thumb strokes the underside of my jaw as he

leans forward and skims his lips on the shell of my ear. "God, you are so much more than we thought."

"We?" I breathe out.

I gasp when he pushes his tongue inside my ear and I feel the hard bulge of his cock pressing against me. "We are few but we are many. Remember that. There are eyes and ears all over this place and we miss nothing. Tread carefully, *psycho*." My mind reels at the use of the name psycho but he short circuits my thoughts when he bites down on my lobe, drawing a pained cry from me. Before I can shove him off me or do anything, he thrusts his hips and I whimper. "Be ready."

"For what?" I stutter.

"To be hunted," he purrs, then pushes off me and waltzes out of my cell with a swagger I have only ever seen mob bosses pull off in movies. When the door clicks shut behind him, I slouch into the bed and release an exasperated sigh.

"I'm so fucked," I mutter into the empty room.

THIRTEEN

DRAVEN

We allow her to think she has a chance of escaping us, but what she doesn't know is she is heading in the direction we want her to. Carter and I slow our pace, allowing her the illusion of being free of us. We are all wearing our own masks tonight. We know Vaughn dropped enough hints for her to figure out who they are but until she admits that shit out loud, we'll keep playing this game of chase the psycho.

She heads down the stairs toward the morgue. We stop at the top of the stairs and allow her a head start. Carter pushes his mask up and faces me. "Bet you my ten soup packets Vaughn locks her in the fridges."

I push my mask up and grin at the fucker. "Bet you my twelve ramen packets he straps her to the table and scares the shit out of her with his knife, then fucks her."

He extends his hand to me with a smile. I place mine in his and shake it before we push our masks down and rush down the stairs to see who is the winner. I start whistling because I know the sound grinds on Carter's nerves and getting under his skin is something I fucking love doing.

When we enter the morgue both of us come to a sudden halt at the sight of Karley on her knees with Vaughn standing in front of her, a gun pressed to her forehead and an old school video camera in his other hand.

This was not the fucking plan.

We were only meant to scare her and fuck with her. Fucking her is a bonus none of us saw coming but we also won't stop.

"What's going on?" Carter asks.

Karley slowly raises her hands and tilts her head back enough to meet Vaughn's mask-covered face. "What do you want me to say?" she asks, ignoring Carter's question.

He and I exchange a look, then look back at her and Vaughn. "I want you to beg daddy to come and save you. Tell him what we have been doing to you," Vaughn barks.

I wait for her to protest, beg and plead for us to let her go, but it seems this girl is in the habit of surprising us at every turn.

"What do I get out of it?" The cocky lilt to her voice has a smirk tugging at the corners of my lips. The girl is either stupid for challenging Vaughn or smart as fuck for seeing there is no way out of this, so she may as well make the best of a fucked-up situation. Carter moves and stops behind her, stretches his arm out and grips her chin from behind, forcing her head back so she is looking up at him.

"You get unlimited access to our cocks and the right to continue breathing." His tone is suggestive and judging from the way she shivers, she is loving what he's putting down but I'm not sold.

"What guarantee do we have that you aren't trying to play us to get daddy dearest to finish the job he started with all of us years ago." She pulls free of Carter's hold and looks at me, a sly smirk tugs at the edge of her face.

"If I was going to fuck you all over, I could do it at any time," she answers.

"You don't have the power," I snap back.

"Knowing who you really are behind the masks gives me that power, so do you want to rethink the statement or should we all agree that we have something to gain out of this little partnership here?" She looks from me to Carter and then finally settles her gaze on Vaughn. "Call me crazy, but I feel you are the one who calls the shots and it seems I need you to agree."

"Why would I do that?" he presses.

Within a split second, tears mist her eyes and her bottom lip begins to tremble. A distraught look enters her eyes and she begins to shake as if she is terrified. "Daddy, please! Get me out of here, give them what they want so they will stop hurting me!" My fucking jaw hits the floor. She swipes her tears away and smiles wide, that fucking performance could have won her a fucking Oscar.

"Well, the bitch had me fooled," I admit.

She looks at me and shoots me a wink. "I aim to please, big boy." Carter chokes on fucking air at her remark, this girl is way too fucking comfortable and clearly just as fucked in the head as us. She has a gun pointed at her and she is smiling. "So, are we in agreement?" she asks Vaughn.

The fucker lifts his head and looks at me and Carter. We all stand here silently for a moment, trying to weigh our options. This girl just showed us she is a master manipulator.

"You have no idea what we have planned—"

She cuts me off before I can continue. "I don't need to. I just need your word that my father will atone for his sins. What he has done—no, what he allows to happen in this place is fucking barbaric and downright disgusting. I don't care what you do to him, I just want him to pay for his crimes."

"Why the fuck would you care about a bunch of washed up has-beens sent here to be forgotten and die," Carter snarls. Much like me, he and Vaughn want vengeance for the crimes lobbed against us. I'm no fucking saint and never have claimed to be. The reason I ended up in here was... I push that train of thought away, knowing it won't serve me any good to pick at that old fucking scab.

Her face morphs, her eyes burn with outrage. "No one should die alone or be treated like this. Fucking dogs are treated better. I'm no God lover but even I know that fucker wouldn't forgive anyone who treated people like this. It's wrong and..." She clamps her mouth closed and drops her gaze to the ground.

Vaughn growls and pushes his gun harder against her forehead. "You know something don't you?"

She gnaws on her bottom lip and slowly flicks her eyes up to meet his stare. "Why would I trust you?"

Vaughn crouches down in front of her and just remains there silently assessing her for a moment before he asks, "Who am I?"

She tilts her head to the side and smiles seductively before reaching out and trailing a single finger down his mask.

"Any chance you will be fucking me with the mask on, *Vaughn,*" she purrs suggestively. Dark laughter fills the morgue as Vaughn pushes his mask up and confirms her suspicions. A self-satisfied smirk graces her face for a second before Vaughn's laughter cuts off. He grips her throat in one hand and pushes the gun against her temple.

"Listen to me, you little cunt. You think because you know my name, my face and what mask I choose to wear that you have an upper hand on us?" He doesn't give her a chance to answer. "Think again. You are a tool we will exploit to draw your father out and when we finally do get him, you will be worth nothing to us. You will be nothing but a distant memory for us and maybe if you are lucky, every couple of months or so, we may think about the taste of your pussy but we'll sure as hell forget what the fuck you looked like, because you mean nothing to us."

FOURTEEN

KARLEY

His words are like a slap to the face. I have let these masked freaks touch me, fuck me and *taste* me. I knew from the first night that whatever may transpire between us would be complicated but I never thought that I would be the only one to feel something. Outside these walls my wants and desires are frowned upon, no sane man would give me everything I crave—*need*— in the bedroom.

At first I never put it together who was behind the other two masks but after hearing their voices, it wasn't hard for me to know Vaughn and Carter were the other two.

"Well while you exploit me, fuck me, demand my submission, I will be here figuring out what it is about you three that has you so hell bent on using me to get to my father." I can see it in Vaughn's eyes, there is a darkness that lurks beneath the surface, his vendetta against my father runs deeper than him being locked in here. Something happened between them and I will figure it out, no matter the cost.

"You talk too fucking much." I peer to my left and smirk.

"Is that right, *Carter*?" His eyes narrow behind the mask, it may have taken me longer than I would have liked to figure out who these two were but at least now we are all on even ground for the time being.

"Knowing our names and faces doesn't change what we have in store for you," he replies without skipping a beat.

"Does my fate involve your face between my legs again?" Draven chuckles darkly to my other side but I ignore him as I focus on Carter, the only way I am going to get the answers I need is by getting under their skin and forcing them to become sloppy so that they spill all their secrets.

The fact I know they can get me off is a bonus.

But, an even bigger bonus is knowing I can get all *three* of them off.

My head is yanked back, drawing a hiss of pain from me. I glare up at Draven who still has strands of my hair tangled in his fingers. "Get the fuck up and lose the clothes." I obey without complaint, forcing Vaughn to lower the gun and climb to his feet. The feeling of all their eyes on me, making me their sole focus, is heady and intoxicating. Once I'm standing before them in nothing aside from my bra and panties, I take a step back so I can have a clear view of all of them. I slowly unclasp my bra and allow the straps to ease down my arms at a snail's pace. Draven and Carter push their masks up so they rest on the tops of their heads, allowing me to see all their faces for the first time.

"Take the panties off and hand them to me," Vaughn growls. I push them down my legs and just to be a little shit, I bundle the material in my hand, then slide it through my slick folds, making sure to get them nice and wet before I stalk forward and drop them into the palm of Vaughn's hand. The hungry look in his eyes contradicts his words from moments ago. All three of them are fucking sexy and I'm not gonna lie, I'm drenched for them.

Vaughn lifts my panties to his nose and inhales deeply before a groan slips past his sinful lips. "Fuck, she smells edible," he says to the guys.

"I need to taste her," Draven grits out, then darts forward, grips me around the waist and lifts me. I wrap my legs around his waist and hold his gaze as he walks. I hiss when he places me on the edge of the table in the morgue, the cold metal burning my sensitive skin. "Open those fucking legs and show me that cunt." I do exactly as he says and unlock my legs from around his waist. I lift my legs until my heels balance on the edge of the table, making sure they get a good view of my dripping wet pussy. "Fucking dirty slut," he purrs, before he drops to his knees in front of me, my nipples instantly hardening as desire courses through me like an inferno.

I lock eyes with Carter as Draven buries his face between my legs and swipes his tongue through my slit, drawing a sharp cry from me. Draven reaches up and cups my tits in his massive hands, then proceeds to swirl his tongue around my clit, making me cry out in pleasure.

"Suck my cock," Vaughn snaps. My eyes widen as Carter turns his back to me and obeys the asshole. Vaughn stares directly at me as Carter begins to lower his pants and free his cock. Before I can even get a glimpse of his dick, it disappears inside Carter's mouth, causing me to pout. "Don't worry, psycho, I won't be coming down his throat. I'm gonna come inside that pussy." His words draw a moan from me.

The sight of Carter's head bobbing up and down

on Vaughn's dick is like a fantasy brought to life. I peer down at Draven and I'm met with the sight of his mask atop his head. Without waiting for permission, I grab the mask from him, causing him to stop and look up at me. I hold his stare as I ease the mask on. I may be fucking insane because the instant the mask is in place I feel a rush of power thrum through me. This mask could be the key to finally embracing who I truly am and allowing all my wants and needs to become a reality and not a dream.

Before I can get too lost in my thoughts, Vaughn and Carter suddenly appear on either side of me. I look from side to side, trying to gauge their expressions and wondering if I just crossed some invisible line, but the second Carter's eyes darken and lust begins to shine in his bright blue eyes, I know the sight of me in this mask is making them feel things they didn't bank on.

I scream out when Draven sucks my clit into his mouth. Vaughn leans down and sucks my nipple into his mouth, drawing a long moan from me. He makes sure to scrape his teeth along my hardened nub and mix pleasure with pain.

Carter pushes the mask off me, then drops it to the ground, my mind a mess thanks to the other two working me into a frenzy.

"You like them touching you?" Carter asks. I nod. His face contorts in anger, his hand grips my throat, constricting my airway, causing my eyes to bulge. Before I can utter a single word, he slaps me with his other hand. I want to balk and fight, knowing rationally I should, but that slap mixed with the feelings the others are forcing me to feel only heightens my desire. "Use your fucking words, bitch," he grits out, then slaps me again but this time I moan, causing a smile to tug at the edges of his mouth.

"Yes. I love feeling their mouths on my cunt and sucking on my nipples, *but*... I love the mix of pain you add to it," I pant out. My words seem to unlock something inside him because his hold on my throat loosens and an unreadable look enters his eyes as he stares at me. Before I can make sense of his look, he smashes his lips against mine. I open for him instantly and melt at the taste of his cool, minty breath. My orgasm rises like a tidal wave ready to wipe an entire city and I wait for Draven to deny me like he did last time, but then Vaughn speaks.

"Make her come on your face." I could almost weep at his mercy, but manage to rein myself in and get lost in the feeling of Draven eating my pussy and Carter tongue fucking my mouth as Vaughn pinches my nipples. "I want you to scream so fucking loud you wake Frank from the dead."

I'm fucked in the head.

Instead of his words causing me to clamp up and tuck tail and run, they have the opposite effect. The orgasm rips through me like a forest fire without warning. I break the kiss with Carter, throw my head back and scream so loud I fear I will wake the fucking dead. Draven doesn't take pity on me and stop sucking on my clit, if anything my screams only seem to encourage him to keep going. I try to push his head away, but Carter and Vaughn grip my arms and force me backward until I'm flat on the table, shaking from my release.

"Please... I can't... Fuck!" I scream out as they begin to strap my wrists to the table. I try to kick out and push Draven away as tears begin to cloud my vision, but those fuckers just grab my legs and hold them still, allowing Draven to continue to torture me. "Stop, please."

"Your mouth says no but your pussy gushing all over his chin says *yes,* so be a good little whore and ride his fucking face until you come again so I can fill that dirty little cunt with my cock!" Carter shouts over my screams.

The chaplain's dirty fucking mouth is my undoing.

Forgive me father for I plan to sin with the therapist, chaplain and inmate and feel no guilt about it because having their cocks in every one of my holes is going to be worth spending eternity in hell burning.

FIFTEEN
CARTER

Her screams bounce off the walls, the scent of her cum stains the morgue like a perfume. I inhale, savoring the sweet smell, my cock rock hard and pressing painfully against my pants. I'm about to rip Draven away from her so I can bury my dick inside her, but he moves without being prompted. Without any warning, I move in front of him and lick her cum from his chin and moan at the taste of her. The fucker grips the back of my neck and smashes his mouth on mine, his tongue forcing my lips open, and when the taste of her hits my taste buds, I groan.

"You like watching us, don't you?" Vaughn asks her as I break the kiss and turn to see her looking directly at us with lust filled eyes.

"Yes," she answers without hesitation. "God, I

fucking love it." The hunger in her tone is clear. Unable to hold back any longer, I move to stand between her legs and push my pants down enough to free my cock. She whimpers at the sight of it, making me smile.

"When you come, I want to hear you scream Draven's name so he knows what it sounds like to hear you scream his name." Draven snorts from behind me. Karley frowns, clearly not getting my jibe at my brother. I grip my dick and run it through her slick folds, loving the feeling of her juices covering my dick and how she trembles with need. Without giving her any warning, I thrust inside her. She cries out and arches her back off the table. Her tits look good enough to eat and my mouth waters with the need to taste them, but I manage to refrain. She tries to tug her arms free but she won't be able to. This table has held all three of us while we got fucked by each other and none of us have been able to break the restraints.

Vaughn moves until he is by her head, his cock in line with her mouth. Without being prompted, she turns toward him and opens her mouth, begging him without words to fill her with the taste of him. Vaughn grins as he grips his cock and begins to stroke himself. She whimpers as I thrust into her ruthlessly.

Her moans are cut off when Vaughn slides his cock between her lips, his head dropping back as a groan rumbles from him. Draven moves to stand behind Vaughn and grips his waist.

I slow my pace to allow Karley a chance to drink in the sight of my guys. Draven uses his hips to push Vaughn in and out of her mouth. Vaugn lolls his head back onto Draven's shoulder, allowing him control. Draven craves control and Vaughn handing over the reins is him showing Draven that he trusts him. Our dynamic may be uncouth and frowned upon by every other motherfucker, but to us, this is just normal. This is our dysfunctional family and we never had plans to allow anyone else to join in on our fun because no one would be able to handle our cravings, but... Karley seems to be handling all three of us.

"Hmmm," she moans as I begin to move inside her again. I watch as Draven grips Vaughn's chin and turns his head to the side, so he can capture his lips in a kiss. I watch her as she watches them, and the way her eyes roll back into her head as she drinks in the sight of them making out has my cock twitching inside her. Drawing her eyes to me, the challenge I see in them has me drawing out of her and stepping back. Her eyes widen but she can't speak. I move across the room to one of the trolleys and pull the top drawer open, but freeze when I hear her scream. I whirl around to find Vaughn fucking her and Draven preparing to shove his cock down her throat. I snatch the tube of lube out of the drawer and stalk back over to them.

Vaughn shoots me a wink as he continues to fuck her *hard*. Draven mutes her cries of pleasure as he pushes his dick inside her mouth, causing her to gag around his large fucking girth. The sinister fucker just smirks, he loves making us gag, the sound of it gets him off and boosts his ego like you wouldn't believe.

I lift the tube of lube to show them both. Instantly they withdraw from her, the sound of her whimper has me grinning.

"Don't pout, you little slut," I growl. The sight of her spit sliding down the edge of her mouth only fuels my desire. "Uncuff her," I order the guys. They do as I say without complaint. Draven grips her shoulders and helps her to sit up. I step forward, forcing my way between her legs and cup the back of her head. She fists the front of my shirt and pulls me in until I'm flush against her.

"Are you going to make me beg, Carter?" The sultry sound of her voice and hearing my name tumble from her lips has the sinner inside me wanting to come out and play. I may ask for forgiveness daily, but the choices I make ensure I will never be able to walk through those pearly gates and be embraced by God himself. If my penance is to remain here on earth with my cock buried in one of my guys' asses or inside her pussy... I can get on board with spending eternity in damnation.

I tighten my hold on the back of her neck, making her wince as I lean forward and ghost my lips over hers. "I'm going to make you wish that you never offered us your body. We're going to use every inch of you and mark you as ours." I don't bother waiting for a reply as I look at the guys. "One on the table." Vaughn kicks his pants off and removes his shirt, exposing the tattoo on his chest. Karley's jaw unhinges.

"What the fuck," she breathes out. Vaughn looks down at his chest and tenses, encased in an inferno of flames is his last name. "Why the fuck do you have that name on your chest?" she presses.

He slowly lifts his head band meets her stare with a scowl so intense she shifts into me further. "Knowing who I am behind the mask isn't my biggest secret," he answers cryptically. Then climbs onto the table behind her, effectively ending the conversation. She opens her mouth ready to push him further on the matter, but Draven cuts in before she can.

"Ride him while Carter gets your ass and I get that filthy mouth around my cock." Heat surges in her eyes, her hundreds of questions for Vaughn are forgotten as her need for release overcomes her rational thought. She spins around and awkwardly crawls up his body until she is straddling him. She reaches down and grips his dick, drawing a hiss from my brother, and lines him up with her pussy, but before she sinks down onto him she says,

"I'm letting the subject of that tattoo drop for tonight because the need to have the three of you filling me is overwhelming my every thought, but don't think for a second that I won't be searching for answers come tomorrow."

"Fuck me good enough and you just might get the answers you want without needing to do any of the dirty work," Vaughn replies. Unable to hold off any longer, I climb onto the metal slab behind her, prompting her without words to hurry the fuck up. She sinks down on Vaughn, slowly moaning as she takes every fucking inch of his cock inside her. Draven growls his approval as he strokes himself. I push her flat against Vaughn and squirt the lube over her asshole and my cock, making sure to lather my cock really good.

When I start to push inside her she tenses, but doesn't ask me to stop. The urge to slam inside her is strong but I manage to hold back and go slow for her benefit. Normally when I fuck one of the guys, there is no mercy, but with her, the urge to take care and make sure she is safe and feels good is so fucking strong it constricts my chest.

To her, we are nothing but strangers but to us, we all feel like we know her better than ourselves. We may be locked in this hell but that doesn't mean we don't have resources and ways to garner information on people outside of here. Just like how we got every bit of intel on her that we needed before finally bringing her here.

SIXTEEN

KARLEY

I scream so fucking loud when Carter plunges the remainder of the way inside my ass, my pussy clamps down on Vaughn, trying to milk him of everything. I had my doubts about us all fitting on this metal slab but somehow they are making it work. I reach out and grip Draven's cock and begin to pump him as I grind down on Vaughn and push back against Carter—I feel so fucking full.

When Carter pulls back, only leaving the tip of his cock in my ass, I want to whimper, but then he thrusts forward roughly and forces a scream of ecstasy from my lips. My clit is throbbing and begging for friction. I push down harder on Vaughn as Carter continues to fuck me. When I feel Vaughn's hot mouth wrap around my nipple, a scream so primal tears out of me as pleasure rocks through every inch of my body.

"Fucking suck my cock, you bitch," Draven snaps. I turn my head to the side and try to take him in my mouth, but I can't reach and my frustration of not being able to have all three of them at the same time mounts. As if sensing my frustration, Draven tears out of my hold and moves to grab a stool.

"Does her pussy feel as good as her ass?" Carter pants.

Vaughn meets his stare over my shoulder, the look of hunger in his eyes fuels me to slam down harder on his cock and take control from both of them as Draven climbs onto the stool. "She's so fucking tight, her cunt is strangling my dick," he answers as I wrap my lips around Draven's cock and swallow him all the way into the back of my throat, loving the taste of him coating my tongue.

When his fingers tangle in my hair and he claims control from me, I surrender.

I force my jaw to relax and my body to go lax as I allow them to take control band give me everything they have. I need this. I need them to unleash their fucking demons on me and use my body.

Draven pushes his cock into my cheek, then slaps my face. I gasp, then choke as he uses my moment of surprise against me and pushes himself further down my throat. Spit drips down my chin and tears leak from my eyes, but the feelings Carter and Vaughn are forcing me to feel numbs my mind until Draven pinches my nose, blocking me from breathing. I try to pull back but a hand clamps down on the back of my neck and holds me in place. I shake my head, trying to break free but none of the guys stop moving. Only when I begin to truly fear that I am going to suffocate does Draven release me and pull his cock from my mouth.

I drag in a lungful of air but Vaughn chooses that moment to thrust inside me and I cry out, the sound so animalistic and primal. Before I can prepare myself an orgasm so powerful rips through me, stealing what little breath I have from my lungs. Black spots dance in the corners of my eyes and I prepare myself to pass out, but I'm snapped out of it when Draven grips my hair. I cry out in pain but the sound is muted when he shoves his cock down my throat again.

"Fucking take my dick like a good little slut," Draven growls. I moan in response as I bob my head up and down on Draven's dick, moaning as I meet the other two thrust for thrust.

"Yes, like that, bitch. I'm gonna come down that

fucking pretty throat," Draven praises. His words spur me on and the urge to please him consumes me, it's as if my only focus in life is pleasing him. I hollow my cheeks and take him deeper than I did before. The groan that comes from him sends a shiver down my spine. Vaughn is fucking me so hard I swear I can feel him hitting my cervix. Before I have time to really enjoy it, Draven throws his head back and roars as he comes down my throat. I swallow every fucking drop of his cum without needing to be prompted.

He tries to pull back but I fist his shirt, holding him in place as I clean his cock and make sure to lick every inch of him clean, savoring the taste as I do. His eyes meet mine and I see raw hunger in their depths.

"Fuck!" I cry out when Carter thrusts inside me so hard Vaughn grunts.

"I'm gonna come in your tight little ass and mark it as mine, you dirty slut," Carter vows.

"Yes!" I answer.

"Yes fucking what?" he snaps.

"Yes please, sir. Fill my ass with your cum," I beg.

"The bitch likes this." Vaughn grunts. I sit up and lean back against Carter, resting my head against his shoulder. His hand wraps around my throat and squeezes. Without his permission I seal my lips against his, loving the shocked look in his eyes as I push my tongue in his mouth.

Vaughn cups my tits in his hands as I bounce up and down on their cocks, chasing another release. The three of us move in sync.

"I'm gonna come," I shout. Vaughn twists my nipples, making me scream. Carter grips my waist and increases his speed. Three more thrusts and then the three of us explode in unison, their carnal roars filling the room followed by my cries of pleasure. Needing to feel the full effect of my release, I lift off Vaughn and squirt all over his abs.

Once I manage to stop shaking from the aftershocks, I unscrunch my eyes and look down to see him staring up at me in shock. It's only then do I realize how fucking quiet the room is. I peer over my shoulder to find Carter's gaze focused on the mess I made on Vaughn. Draven is staring at me like I am the missing piece to a puzzle. Panic begins to unfurl inside me.

"I'm sorry," I blurt, then try to move off Vaughn but Carter's grip on me tightens.

"What the fuck was that?" Vaughn hisses. I cringe in shame and drop my gaze.

"It won't happen again," I mutter.

He grips my chin and forces my gaze to his, anger swirling in his eyes and I mentally curse myself for ruining this moment. "The fuck you mean it won't happen again?" he hisses.

"I... I mean–I won't do it again," I manage to say.

"Yes, yes the fuck you will!" Draven snaps.

My brows furrow in confusion. "Huh?"

"Why the fuck didn't you squirt when we first ate you out?" Carter barks.

"Ah, I didn't want to gross you out," I admit.

"You dumb bitch," Draven says and shakes his head.

"You being able to squirt is one of the fucking hottest things and I plan to make you do it every time we fuck you," Vaughn adds.

"In fact, I'm about to switch places with Vaughn right now and you are going to come all over my dick," Carter announces as he eases out of my ass.

My eyes widen in surprise. "Seriously?" I press.

"Get the fuck off my dick now so you can suck your cum off me before Carter gets to feel how fucking amazing it is to have your cum all over him." Vaughn's praise emboldens me. I shift down his body and situate myself on my hands and knees between his legs and suck his dick. I moan around his length when Draven slips behind me and buries his face in my pussy. Knowing that the three of them are going to spend their days making me squirt has me trembling with excitement. No man has ever been able to make me do that before, only I have made myself do it, so watching them fight for the right to own every single one of my releases is going to be better than getting forgiveness from God himself.

SEVENTEEN

VAUGHN

It has been over a month since Karley arrived here, the girl is proving to be more than we thought possible. As the days turned to weeks, a part of me started to feel guilty for what we were doing to her. I know Carter and Draven are growing feelings for her and that shit is dangerous. I told them to keep their feelings out of this but they never stood a chance against her. The bitch is like a vortex, she sucks you in and there isn't a fucking thing you can do to fight it.

Every night when the doors open and that buzzer sounds, we hunt.

We have chased her through every inch of this place and fucked her on more surfaces than we can count. We have pushed her boundaries and forced her out of the cage she kept herself in just to see how far we can push her before she finally breaks.

What she doesn't know is that I have been recording every encounter.

Every sound she has made.

Every orgasm we have wrung from her.

Each time we have come on her and marked her as ours.

Every moment has been recorded and sent to her father.

In each of those videos we are all wearing our masks—only after I have stopped recording do we remove them. She tries to pretend she doesn't like the masks and that us hunting her each night doesn't get her off, but every time we feel her rotten little cunt, it's always drenched and ready for us.

I bite back a groan at the memory of how she felt last night, the way she rode me while taking Draven in her ass and Carter in her mouth had me blowing my load so fucking hard and deep inside her cunt.

"Draven moved her into his room last night." I whirl around and face Carter with wide eyes. The fucker chuckles at my expression and nods. "Yeah, I had the same fucking reaction when I saw him moving all of her shit."

"Since when is he okay with sharing his fucking space? He didn't even want to share with us!"

"You sound like a jealous girlfriend, Vaughn," Carter snarks, earning a glare from me.

"That son of a bitch has never spent the night with us, yet he wants that fucking bitch with him full time. You both need to get your fucking heads checked because she is the reason we are fucking here!" I roar.

Carter's eyes narrow, he crosses the room and stands before leaving a sliver of space between us. I can feel the anger wafting off him and the tension in the air is tangible but I'm not fucking backing down. These asshole's knew she was a means to an end and now they have gone and caught fucking feelings for her and it is complicating this whole situation.

"She had nothing to do with the fucking predicament we are in," he defends her.

"Yes the fuck she does!"

He grips the front of my shirt and pulls me in so our foreheads are touching. "She isn't her father, Vaughn."

I close my eyes and take a shuddering breath. I know my anger is misdirected and none of this is Carter or Draven's fault, but the closer we get to bringing her father down the more unhinged I am becoming because I want out of this fucking place. I've lost everything because of that cunt she calls a father, he ruined my life.

Carter grips the back of my neck and stares directly into my eyes. "I know what this means for you. We all do, but you need to understand that she isn't her father. She didn't put us here. Take a minute to watch her and observe her. She cares about us and this palace. She tries to help others and treats them with kindness."

I snort. "Kindness? That girl doesn't show an ounce of that shit when we are fucking her nightly." We both chuckle, but it's forced. The tension is still thick and Carter knows I'm strung out.

"Tonight. You need to hunt her... *alone.*" I jerk back and stare at him like he has lost his fucking mind. I open my mouth to argue but he beats me to it. "You need to see she isn't who you have made her out to be. She isn't him, Vaughn. Tonight, take the time to really see her and let her show you she isn't a monster."

The second the doors open, I pull my mask down and inhale deeply. I've fucked this bitch every night for the past month yet this night, it feels different. Unlike the other times, I am going into this with expectations. When Draven walks into our room with his mask in place I know he isn't going to accept sitting out tonight easily.

"He needs to do this on his own," Carter says.

Draven pushes his mask up and looks between the two of us before finally settling his gaze on me. Whatever he sees in my eyes has him nodding and stepping out of the doorway.

"She's gone out the back." I nod and move to step past him, but he places a hand on my chest, halting my escape. "Don't fucking break her," he warns.

I look at him, like really look at him, and that's when I see the truth in his eyes. "You're in love with her." It isn't a question and he doesn't justify my claim with an answer, just drops his arm back to his side and allows me to leave. As I leave the room, I suddenly feel like the weight of the world is on my shoulders. For the first time since solidifying this bond between me, Carter and Draven, I don't know if they would choose me. She has a leash around their necks and she doesn't even know it.

I make it out the back in record time and prepare

to chase her down, but what I don't expect to see is her standing in the middle of the ruined basketball court looking directly at me. Her eyes hold mine, no words are exchanged, they aren't needed in this moment.

"*When the devils come for their prey there is no escape. The torture they inflict is depraved and ungodly. No amount of prayers to your make-believe God will make them stop,*" she says quietly.

"Who told you that?" I grit out.

She shrugs. "Draven."

I nod, that does sound like something that twisted fuck would tell her. "You should run," I say as I take a step forward. She shakes her head and crosses her arms over her chest.

"What's the point in running from something that I want?" Her question floors me and forces me to still my movements. "I want this," she adds to drive her point home.

"All you want is three cocks buried inside your pussy every night because it's your way of saying fuck you to Daddy."

She flinches at my words. "If that were true, I wouldn't be here."

"You didn't have a choice."

"If all I wanted was to say fuck you to my dad, then I wouldn't have had to use my body to do that."

"Your body is ours to do with as we please." She closes the space between us and stops an inch away, craning her head back to keep her eyes locked on mine.

"If I told you I didn't want this, would you stop or would you force me?" My face slackens, I grind my teeth so hard my jaw begins to ache. I remain silent. I could lie and tell her that I would force myself upon her every night but she would know that's a lie. "If all you wanted was to hurt him, then you would have used me to do that. You want me as much as I want *you*. Yet, you refuse to admit that to yourself."

I stand here with bated breath, waiting for him to acknowledge that he feels something for me. Draven and Carter may not have uttered the words aloud but they have shown me with their touch, how they react when I am around, or how they constantly have to touch me and keep me near them.

Vaughn, on the other hand, is always reserved, held back and brooding in the corner unless he's sinking his cock in me. It's only then does he allow his mask to fall and give me a glimpse into the real him. He may never utter the words or show me with his touch, but his eyes tell me everything his mouth can't.

He feels something for me!

He reaches out and wraps his hand around my

ponytail, tugging on the strands, drawing a hiss of pain from me. He leans down until the rough texture of his mask scrapes against my skin, sending desire pooling between my legs.

"Sinking my cock inside your dirty little cunt doesn't mean I give a fuck about you." I gasp at his callous words. "Carter and Draven may pine after you but not me... you are a means to an end and some new toy we get to play with so we can pass the time quicker." Tears prick the backs of my eyes but I blink them away, refusing to allow him to see how much his words affect me. I push him back. If he didn't want to move he wouldn't have but he's allowing me the space I need right now.

"Why can't you just admit you like me?" I yell.

His answering chuckle has me clenching my fists at my sides as I try to tamper down my rage. "Why the fuck would I lie just to appease your self-worth?"

I throw my hands in the air, growing frustrated. "It isn't about my self-worth, Vaughn, it's about the fact I'm falling in—" I clamp my mouth closed and turn my back to him, I can't believe I nearly let those words slip free. What the fuck would someone like me know about love anyway? It's not like I had a mother to show me how it feels to be loved. My dad has always been about himself and his bank account.

The second I feel his heat at my back, I melt into him. His hands encase my waist, making me feel safe. I've never felt safe or protected in my life until I met these three. They make me feel wanted, cherished and cared for. Vaughn may be the last to admit his feelings but I know he cares about me.

When his grip on my waist turns punishing, I flinch. "Tonight is your last night, psycho." His tone holds a cold edge to it but there is a hint of something else there that I can't put my finger on. I peer over my shoulder at him.

"Last night for what?" I ask quietly.

"To have us. I should have told them the truth, but when he offered me to have you to myself, I chose to remain silent."

My eyes widen in surprise. "I get you... alone?"

"Do your worst, psycho," he baits me.

"Put your hands on my body, Vaughn, and show me without words that you own me," I throw back at him. The animalistic growl that rumbles out of him brings a smile to my face. "Show me how much you want my pussy," I add as I spin around in his hold. He grips the backs of my thighs and lifts me. I wrap my arms and legs around him as he walks us toward the wooded area where they caught me that first night. It feels like so long ago, how can it only have been weeks?

I may be a prisoner here, yet I have never felt so free.

None of the other inmates have bothered me. When the doors open they know to stay out of my way or the guys will be there to punish them for touching what's theirs. I shiver at the thought of watching Draven beat the shit out of one guy. He thought I was alone and had no idea the guys were hunting me. The second he grabbed me, Draven appeared out of nowhere. Draven beat him within an inch of his life, then made me suck him off next to the unconscious guy. He wouldn't allow me to swallow his release. Instead, he blew his load all over the guy, marking him as their property. Call me crazy but I lost my shit because their cum belongs to me and no one else. That night, they all took their time with me and made sure I knew that they were mine.

Well, everyone except Vaughn.

I cry out in pain when he slams me against a tree. I glare down at him. "What the fuck?" I hiss.

"You have gotten too comfortable with thinking you call the shots. Tonight I'm going to remind you that we are the ones who are in control." I moan in anticipation. He draws his hips back then thrusts forward allowing me to feel his hard length pressed against my core. He shifts so he can push his hand inside my sweats. I reach for his mask, wanting to see his face but he shakes his head. "Tonight you get fucked by the devil."

My train of thought is short circuited when he presses the pad of his thumb against my clit. I cry out. "Fuck," I rasp out when he slides his fingers lower. I tense when I feel him tug on the string of my tampon. My eyes widen in shame, I forgot all about it! "We have to stop, I'm on my period."

He scoffs. "You think a little blood is going to stop me from eating and fucking this cunt?"

My eyes widen. "What?"

"I'm interested to know where you got tampons from?"

"Carter." He snorts and nods, then tugs on the string, pulling it out. I balk when he holds it up between our faces. I want to shrink and hide, never in my life did I ever think a guy would not be bothered by the fact I'm on my period and still want me. Most guys would turn and tuck tail, but not this guy. Vaughn tosses it over his shoulder, lowers me to my feet, then he drops to his knees before me and tugs my pants down. I kick them to the side and wait to see what he does next.

"Throw your leg over my shoulder and show me that bloody cunt." I suck in a sharp inhale at his crass words, but do as he says.

"That's a sight I love to see. I can't wait to have your blood all over my face and cock." I open my mouth to... I don't know what the fuck I was going to say but the words die on my tongue when he pushes his mask up onto the top of his head, then sinks his tongue into my tight hole, forcing a scream out of me.

"Holy shit," I cry out when he grips the globes of my ass and pulls me in closer. My body moves of its own accord, I begin grinding against his face, chasing my release. The fact he has no reservations about eating me out right now has need riding me so hard. I reach down and grip the sides of his face and hold him in place as I use his tongue for my own pleasure.

"Give it to me," he demands, then sucks on my clit as he buries two fingers inside me. My orgasm crashes into me without warning. I scream loud, and I swear I have scared all the wildlife away. Vaughn doesn't bring me down from my high, he withdraws his fingers, then climbs to his feet and stares down at me. The sight of my blood on his chin has my jaw falling open. The bastard smirks as he brings his blood covered fingers to my face and says, "Clean them."

NINETEEN
VAUGHN

I wait for her to refuse me. I want her to so I can punish the bitch. When she leans forward and wraps her lips around my fingers, and licks them clean while whimpering, I nearly come in my fucking pants. This girl isn't like any woman I have known before.

She releases my fingers with a wet pop and to make sure she has proven her point, she presses onto her tiptoes and licks the underside of my chin, cleaning it of her blood.

"I love the taste of me on your skin," she purrs. I snarl in response, then shove her back against the tree. The bitch just smiles and wags her brows, taunting me to take whatever the fuck I want.

"Get my cock out," I bark. She obeys without

complaint. When she wraps her dainty hand around me, I hiss. Before I can enjoy it too much, I bat her hand away and spin her around so her cheek is pressed against the bark of the tree and slap her ass twice. She yelps but doesn't shift from her spot. I step back and grip her hips, forcing her to bend. I give no warning as I plunge my cock inside her. She cries out and the sound of her pleasure mixed with the sting of pain has me shuddering.

"Vaughn," she pants as I draw back, only to thrust inside her once more.

"Scream my fucking name so every cunt knows this is *my* fucking pussy, psycho." Her cunt clamps down on my dick, trying to milk me of everything I have to give.

"Tell me you're mine, Vaughn," she begs as I slam in and out of her, my grip on her hips turning bruising. I fuck her hard and deep, needing this release to curb some of the anger inside me.

She means nothing to you! Don't let her poison your mind.

I repeat that shit over and over again in my head —the more I say it, it will become true. I just need to fuck her out of my system.

"I'm gonna come!" she screams. I increase the speed of my thrusts, making sure she can feel every single inch of my cock as I force the orgasm from her, I need to feel her squirt all over my dick. Every night the guys and I make it our mission to see who can make her squirt the hardest and longest. Tonight, I will be the victor and I will be the only one to feel her come on my cock, and that shit has me ready to fucking explode. "Vaughn!" she screams my name loud enough for everyone inside to hear who she fucking belongs to.

I pull out of her, then force her to her knees and shove my cock in her mouth. She gags around my girth but I give zero fucks, my care factor meter is nowhere to be fucking seen as I chase this release. It isn't a want, it's a fucking *need.* She grips the globes of my ass and pulls me deeper into her mouth and when she swirls her tongue around the underside of my dick, I fucking erupt.

I throw my head back and roar my release, spilling every fucking drop of cum down her sinful throat. Shockwaves pulse through me. I wait for her to release me from the confines of her hot, wet mouth but she doesn't. Instead she kneels before me with her eyes locked on mine and licks my dick clean. I shiver at the sight of her looking like a goddess. She has smears of blood on her cheeks and chin but it doesn't seem to bother her, and that sight alone has me wanting to fuck her again so I can use her own blood as lube as I fuck her ass.

I spend the next couple of hours fucking her in the woods. I've come in her ass, cunt, down her throat and all over her body. We're both fucking filthy and look like a murder scene, but I have never felt so sated and... at ease. I roll off and flop to my back on the ground, the only sounds that can be heard are our ragged breaths.

"I don't think I can move," she admits.

I chuckle and loll my head to the side. She's looking right at me with a sleepy smile. The look on her face has something inside me constricting. I turn away from her, unable to handle the emotions that one look is stirring inside me.

"I gotta go," I grit out. I move to sit up but she grips my arm, forcing me to remain where I am, but I still can't look at her.

"Don't shut me out, please."

I tear my arm free of her hold and stand. I look around for my clothes, only to find her clutching my shirt and pants. I reach down to snatch them from her but she won't let them go.

"Unless you want me to fuck you until you pass out, let go."

She narrows her eyes. "If that's what it takes for you to stop shutting me out, then fine."

"What the fuck do you want me to say, Karley?" I don't give her a chance to answer. "I never lied to you. I told you from the first time we met that you would be used and you have been."

"In case you haven't noticed, I've been willing and all too happy to be a part of your nightly fucking—"

"I've been videoing us fucking you and sending it to your father." Her eyes widen to the size of dinner plates and her jaw slackens at my revelation. "Still want me to stand here and admit my feelings?" I taunt.

Tears fill her eyes as she stares up at me. She releases my pants but pulls my shirt over her head to shield her nakedness from me. I give her a second to mull over my words as I pull my pants on.

"You're lying," she whispers, the hint of hope in her tone only serves to make me angrier.

"No."

The tears begin to run down her cheeks. "I don't believe you," she chokes out as she wraps her arms around her waist, as if she is trying to hold herself together but her eyes drop to the tattoo across my chest.

"You're smart enough to know the reason I have *Slade* tattooed."

She swallows audibly. "Your last name is Slade, isn't it?" It's posed as a question but she already knows the answer.

"Robert and I opened Slade Le Roux together, and for two years everything was great. We were doing well. But then I found out your father was just pocketing the checks from the state every month and never putting anything back into this place or toward the care for the patients. When I confronted that motherfucker, he had me admitted! I have been stuck in here for years because of that selfish cunt." Tears cascade down her cheeks but I'm not done, now that I've started I can't stop. "I want my fucking freedom and for your father to pay for what he's done."

"That's why you hate me," she whispers brokenly.

"You knew my stance on this shit—"

"I didn't expect to fall for the three of you!" she screams. "Jokes on me though, huh?" She doesn't allow me to answer. "While I was falling in love with the devils, you were all exploiting me."

"I told—"

"Shut up!" Sobs tear out of her and for the first time I actually feel guilty for what I've done to her.

"If you had just asked me and explained what had happened, I would have helped you. I would have made sure the three of you were given your freedom."

"How the fuck were you going to do that?" I snap.

"Have you ever asked yourself why I haven't tried to escape or begged any of the nurses for help when they do their piss poor checks every other day?"

My brows bunch as I stare at her. "What?"

She drops her arms back to her sides, her face blank of all emotion and I tense at the hardened look in her eyes. "I hate my father as much as you do! Being here was the first time I have been able to be free of the burden of my last name and not fucking paraded around at galas like a prized fucking cow." She's yelling now and her tears are no longer from heartache but from pent up rage. "I had no idea what the fuck my father was doing here. I didn't even know about this place or how it was being run, yet you still chose to put the blame on me and make me the monster in your story. Newsflash, asshole, I have been a victim to his cruelty my whole fucking life. If you had just told me the truth and trusted in me to be better than my father, I would have helped you."

I stand here and watch her walk away from me as my chest starts to constrict and I feel the wind has been knocked out of me.

I've been fighting my feelings for weeks, only for them to finally surface but now, it's too late, the damage is done and her father is coming for her tomorrow.

TWENTY

KARLEY

When I left Vaughn last night I headed straight for the showers. After I washed the blood away, I dropped to my knees and bawled my fucking eyes out. I'm not the type of girl who sits there and cries over boys, but last night I couldn't stop the tears and sobs from coming.

When I finally dragged my sorry ass back to my room, Draven was nowhere to be seen. I was grateful for that small mercy because I couldn't deal with facing him. Draven may appear hard and emotionless to everyone else, but not to me. He is sweet and kind and always takes note of my sudden mood changes. Carter is attentive and loves to spoil me with affection, but Vaughn, he is the one that has held me at arms' length and never allowed me close.

Waking this morning, I expect to find Draven in his bed but the room is empty.

My chest is tight, this is what I was worried about. I knew the three of them were close. I had worried if Vaughn told them to stay away from me that they would. I fooled myself into thinking I meant more to them than that, but I guess I was wrong. I wasn't just the monster in Vaughn's story, it appears I was the monster in *all* of their stories.

When my door opens, I sit up and stare at the three masked bastards standing in my doorway. Unlike all of the other times, I don't get butterflies. My stomach sinks. Something is wrong and I can feel it with every fiber of my being that my heart is about to be shattered. I was a fucking fool to allow feelings into whatever the hell this is between me and them, but you can't keep fucking the same people over and over and fucking over again without feeling something!

"It's time." They may change their masks but I know the sound of their voices. Carter is wearing Draven's mask, the matte black is peeling and the red lines only add to the gory look.

"Time for what, Carter?" My tone holds a harsh edge but I can't find it within myself to care.

"For the reckoning," Draven adds. I don't move

an inch, if these bastards think I am going to blindly follow them like I have been for weeks, then they have another thing coming. Draven is wearing Vaughn's mask with the snapped horns, leaving Vaughn in Carter's with the large, curved horns.

Vaughn doesn't wait for a response, he marches inside my room and throws me over his shoulder. I kick, punch and scream, but he doesn't falter in his strides as he carries me out into the hallway and takes off toward the staff exit. I've never been past this point and the fact the doors open for them without needing to flash an ID card tells me they have way more power over this place than I originally thought.

"Shut the fuck up!" Vaughn roars. I punch him harder in the back, wanting him to feel as much pain as possible.

"Kiss my ass, you mask wearing fucking freak!" I scream. I cry out when my head is yanked up by my hair and I lock eyes with Carter.

"I pray for forgiveness every day and it is never granted, but I pray that you will forgive us for what is about to happen." I snap my mouth closed, unsure of what the fuck to say to that, but I stop screaming. After being jostled around on Vaughn's shoulder for a few more minutes, he comes to a stop and glides me down the front of his body.

I loathe to admit I savor the feeling of how he feels pressed against me. When I sway on my feet, he grabs my waist to steady me and meets my angry stare. His eyes are blank of all emotion and I hate that I can't get a read on him.

"Your freedom is yours to do with as you please," he says in an even tone, then brushes past me to push the door open. I whirl around and freeze at the sight of my father standing in the room with three other men that I recognize as his lawyers. Dad doesn't even spare me a single glance, he just looks between the three guys and stares at them.

My own father doesn't even care to look at me and see if I'm injured, all he is worried about is ending this so none of my sex tapes are leaked and I ruin the Le Roux name.

"Thatcher," Dad hisses. The man on his right dumps two duffle bags on the flimsy metal table, then draws the zippers back to expose all the cash inside them. My stomach sinks. This was never about feelings for them, this was about using me to get money and to get the hell out of this place.

"I'm a fool," I whisper.

"Speak up, Karley, you know I can't stand it

when you mumble." I flinch at the harsh tone of my father's voice, he has never physically hurt me but emotionally? My father is the champion at emotional manipulation. With his words alone, he can shred you into tiny pieces and make you feel like you are worth less than the dog shit beneath your boot. That is how I have felt my whole life.

"Where's the paperwork?" Vaughn snarls.

Dad's eyes narrow, I know it is driving him crazy not knowing who the three of them are. "Give it to him," Dad orders. Another man steps forward and drops a mahogany colored folder on the table next to the bags. "Now, I want those tapes." I cringe and scrunch my eyes closed.

"We'll be keeping those," Carter says.

I open my eyes to see my father turning a bright shade of red. Robert Le Roux isn't used to not having control, his wealth always makes him the strongest person in the room but not this time.

"We had a deal!" my father yells. I shrink back a step and slam into Draven, who wraps his arm around my waist protectively. In a situation like this I should feel safer with my own kin but I don't. Dad finally meets my stare and the unfiltered hatred I see in his eyes has me defaulting. It never mattered what I did in life, I was always a disap-

"Move!" Robert snaps at her from the doorway, but she doesn't budge. She looks at us like we are strangers, her emotions are walled off but I can still see the pain in the depths of her green eyes.

"I'm so sorry," she mutters after a minute, then drops her gaze. Her shoulders hunch and she turns and follows her father. Standing here and letting her walk away from us is one of the hardest fucking things I have ever had to do. None of us utter a word for a long ass time, each of us are too lost in our own thoughts.

My chest is aching. I hate being away from her already.

I've never wanted to share a space with anyone but I want her to take up every inch inside me. I want to be inside her, see what makes her tick, make myself at home inside her veins, taste her blood and bathe in that shit so she is all around me. Karley Le Roux has left a hole inside me in her absence and there isn't a single fucking soul in this world that will be able to fill that void, aside from her.

"Tell me you got that shit?" Carter asks, finally breaking the silence.

"Every fucking word. We have our freedom, now it's time to take back what he stole from us," Vaughn answers. I move toward the table and open the file to see our release papers and the deed of Slade Le Roux changed to us. We now own this place.

"I thought I would feel different," I admit.

"Me too," Carter adds.

"She will see in time why it had to be this way," Vaughn says resolutely.

"She didn't look at us like she used to." Admitting that shit out loud hurts.

Vaughn sighs and scrubs a hand down his face. "She wouldn't have left with him if we told her the truth."

"How the fuck do you know that?" Carter growls.

Vaughn meets his hardened stare with one of his own. "She would have wanted to stay and fix this shit with us because of what she just learned. She now knows the truth about why we are in here. She thinks we all hate her—"

"You do hate her!" I interject.

Vaughn shakes his head. "I fell in love with that girl weeks before she even arrived here. Pretending that I hated her everyday nearly killed me. If she knew how I really felt, she would have stayed with us because she loves us. She needs to be as far away from us as she can be right now. We are so close to

I use the shampoo and soap that is in the stall and take my time scrubbing every inch of my body. I don't know when the next time I will be allowed to shower, so I'm going to take my time and enjoy this and I do, until the fucking lights shut off. I quickly finish rinsing the shampoo from my hair and shut the shower off.

I strain my hearing, listening for any sounds that someone is in here with me. When I hear the distinct sound of footsteps, dread weaves its way through me. As quietly as I can, I reach out through the shower curtain and try to grab my towel from the hook but I grip nothing but air. Panic sets in and my breathing turns choppy. At Slade Le Roux I knew what I was getting myself into, Draven explained the rules that first night, but here, I'm flying blind.

I take three calming breaths and lift my chin, I'm going to fake this shit until I make it because I won't let this fucking place break me.

"Whoever the fuck you are, you better return my towel now and get the hell out before I scream," I shout. My words bounce off the walls and echo slightly. I wait for a long while and when I hear nothing, I slowly draw the curtain back and gasp at the sight of the neon paint on the mirror. I read the one word three times before it finally sinks in.

Run.

I take off like a bat out of hell for the exit, then pull the door open, expecting to see the nurse but the hallway that was just filled with people is now empty and dark. I can only see a few feet in front of me. Fear is choking me and trying to get me to submit but the demon inside me refuses to cower. If this is one of my dad's sick games, I won't allow him the upper hand. I tread carefully and slowly, I run my fingertips along the wall, using it to help guide me back toward the common area that I have to pass through to get to my room.

Goosebumps prick my skin and the hairs on the back of my neck stand up when I enter the common area. I feel eyes on me. I dart my eyes around but see nothing but blackness. I know I'm not alone, and the fact I have nothing to defend myself with and I'm naked doesn't bode well for me. I pause in the center of the room, feeling a presence in front of me. I feel another behind me and on my right.

I close my eyes and try to garner the strength I'll need to fight my way out of this. Draven isn't here to save me this time from being raped. His reaction makes sense now, why he killed that guy.

"If you want me, you're gonna have to come get

that I was more than a bargaining chip, they showed me how they truly felt about me.

Their hunger for me is insatiable.

After we left, they told me they had my father sign everything over to me. They still won't tell me how they did it and I don't want to know. I am now in charge of the Le Roux fortune and I have done everything I can to fix my father's mistakes. I even found Frank's wife and honored his last wish. We closed Slade Le Roux, but I chose to leave my father locked in there *alone*. He is fed and checked on daily but no one interacts with him. Draven allowed me to make the call on his fate.

I barely think about him now. I visited my father a couple of months after he was locked in there. The way he looked at me with such disgust and hatred only proved that I made the right decision to not allow Draven to end his life. The guys came with me, but stood back and allowed me to take control, that was no easy feat for them.

I told my father how I always felt small around him and how he always made me feel less than I was, weak and unloved. The gleeful look on his face as I confessed to him had me wanting to remove his fucking skin from his body but instead, I hit him where it hurt. I told him how my guys made me feel empowered, loved, cherished and above all else, safe. That stupid smirk vanished from his face and I felt a surge of power rush through me, knowing I was the one that held the key to his fate. When I tried to leave, he begged for his freedom. I refused and was all too happy to let him know he would never get out. He would remain a prisoner of Slade Le Roux forever. He would die there and be forgotten just like he had planned for my guys to be.

The guys keep my mind busy and so does work. Carter, Vaughn and Draven all help me run the care facilities and every night, they hunt me. I shiver as thoughts of last night run through my mind.

Carter fucked me against the pool house, while Vaughn had Draven bent over the lounger—seeing my guys fuck always gets me off. I never last long and they know it. All of them are trying to get me pregnant, they say the sight of me round and swollen with a baby inside me will have them rocking a boner all day long.

"Psycho." I snap my head up from my computer and smile at Vaughn, God he is fucking sexy. I've been waiting for my hunger for them to lessen but if anything, the more time I spend with them has only heightened my need. "If you keep making fuck me

THANK YOU!

Still think the pearly gates are the better option or would you rather burn with the demons?

Thank you so much for reading Dirty Little Psycho, I enjoyed every fucking second of writing this book and diving into each of these crazy bastards' minds and allowing their wants to flow through me.

You reading *Dirty Little Psycho* means the world to me that you have taken a chance on reading one of my books!

STALKER LINKS

Newsletter 
Facebook 
Reader's Group 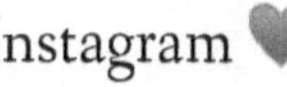
Instagram 
TikTok 
Amazon 
Website 
Bookbub 
Goodreads 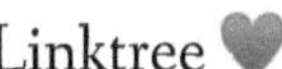
Linktree

Also By Samantha Barrett

Mafia Romance's

https://books.bookfunnel.com/mafiaseries

Secret Society/ Bully/ Masked Men

https://books.bookfunnel.com/dirtytemptation

Sinners Welcome (Pure Smut Novellas)

https://books.bookfunnel.com/sinnerswelcome

Samantha's Entire Backlist

https://books.bookfunnel.com/SamanthasBookverse

ACKNOWLEDGMENTS

Husband, darling how you put up with me each day is a mystery to me. How you embrace my darker side and allow me to try all these positions on you should grant you free access to the pearly gates. Marrying me was the first mistake you made because till death fucking do us part, baby!

MJ & Ray-Ray, the spawn of my baby daddy's loins. The reason I love writing dark romance so much, you two have the power to send me to an asylum by just being you and I fucking love you for it. Embrace who you are and never allow the world to change you because you weren't born to fit in, you were always destined to stand out.

Leah Maree, my evil counterpart, my ride till the motherfucking wheels fall off. I have no words except to say I am always in your debt. Your friendship is always something I will cherish.

My PA, my bestie from another testie, Sarah - fucking - Wilson, you don't need a long novel, you know you are the backbone to this whole thing and I would be fucked without you.

My alpha's, Debbie, Clare, Erin and Samantha (number 2), you four are just as fucking crazy and unhinged as I am and sometimes I wonder if we all need help but honestly, fuck it. The world needs more crazy ass bitches like us.

My beta babes, Taay, Amber, Amanda, Nicole, Patti, Morgan, Alex & Rizzo, thank you ladies for trusting me and being on this rollercoaster of a ride with me, I am forever grateful to each and everyone of you!

My ARC army girls, thank you beautiful souls so fucking much for always sticking by me and trusting me to mend those hearts that I break. I wish I could hug each of you and tell you in person how incredibly grateful I am for you all and one day I hope to be able to do that.

Lizz, how you continue to put up with me and all my random ideas is a fucking mystery I never want to solve! You are the rock to this whole gig and honestly, I wouldn't want to be on this ride with anyone else but you!

My darling dark delicious readers, thank you again for following me and reading each of these books. I cannot tell you how much it means to me that you follow me on this ride and love each of these characters as much as I do.

Sam xxx

ABOUT THE AUTHOR

Samantha Barrett is originally from Auckland, New
Zealand but living in Brisbane, Australia.

Sam writes all things dirty dark and delicious with a
side of twisted mind fuck.

She is a lover of all things red flags and an anti-hero is
a must.